ATLAS

THE GIDEON BROTHERS

BOOK 2

J. NELL

DISCLAIMER

This book cantains material that is only suitable for mature audiences over the age of eighteen yeas of age. Strong language, violence, and explicit sexual content included. Please read the trigger warnings before you proceed! Proceed at your own discretion.

TRIGGER WARNING!
This book contains sensitive material including: Child abuse, domestic violence, sexual assault, grooming, violence, suicide, self-harm, vivid nightmare imagery, substance abuse, childhood trauma, PTSD, graphic violent scenes, sex trafficking.

CHAPTER ONE

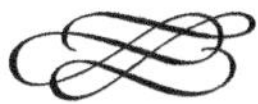

lexander

"ATLAS! WAKE UP!" He opened his eyes, instantly confused. It's after two a.m., and I am in his room with his brothers waking him up. I put my fingers to my mouth, telling him to be quiet. Pulling the covers back, I tell him to get up. I go to the window and open it, looking out to make sure the coast is clear. I call my sons over to the window and kneel in front of Atlas, my oldest son, and tell him to take his brothers down to their aunt and uncle's house. "Atlas, stay out of sight and make sure you get your brothers to your Aunt Bria and Uncle Hemi's house," I say.

"OK, Dad," Atlas says.

"Do not come back here, Atlas. Go straight to your uncle's house, promise me," I say to him.

"I promise, Dad," he says. Atlas is the first one lowered out of the window, followed by my other three sons. I look at my little boys knowing full well that this may be the last time I see them. They stand there looking at me, scared, confused, and cold. There was no time to grab their coats for them. I run back over to the bed and grab the comforter, thankful that Atlas's

favorite color is navy blue. It's dark, so it won't be easy to see. I drop it out of the window. "Hurry," I say to them. "I love you."

"We love you too, Daddy," they say before they start for their uncle's house. I watch them run until they disappear into the shadows. The noises are getting closer. I close the window, pull the curtains together, and make Atlas' bed look just like my other son's beds—like they were never there, and walk out of the room.

Atlas

I wake with a start, tangled in sweat-soaked sheets and shaky hands. Getting up, I head to the bathroom to take a shower and get ready for my day. I've had the same dream for the past thirty-eight years, and I always wake up before finishing it. I wake up at various points in the dream, but no matter what, I never get to the end. I do not have to dream the dream to remember what happened. I was there and will never forget it. Throwing on a pair of jeans, a long sleeve white shirt, and my wheat work boots, I head out into the main house. I am sure Jaasiel has made breakfast. The man is a genius in the kitchen. If he felt like becoming a bonafide chef, he could; he's that good.

I leave my wing of the mansion that I share with my brothers, and I can hear the family talking and laughing as I stride toward the kitchen. Just like I imagined, there is Jaasiel at the stove, and a buffet is set up on our twelve-foot island. Yeah, I know it may sound like that is unnecessarily long, but we are pretty big guys. I am six feet, nine inches tall and three hundred and thirty-five pounds. Only my brother Joshua is bigger at seven feet tall and three hundred and fifty pounds. Joseph comes in right after me, and our youngest brother Jabarri comes in at six feet, four inches tall, and two hundred and thirty-five pounds, and there are eight of us.

So the island is the perfect size for us. I should've said nine of us. I see my sister sitting at the island eating. She is not our blood sister. She is married to Joshua, or Jag, as she calls him. I am so happy he found someone to love him and who he could love. He became another father to us even after he left to go into the service.

I walk up behind Savvy and pluck her off the stool she's sitting on. She screeches as I take her by surprise.

"Atlas!" she yells. "Put me down!"

I know it will only be a matter of seconds before her husband comes to investigate who is bothering his wife. *Five, four, three, two, one...*

"Savvy!" His voice booms from their wing of the house as he rushes out to find out what caused her to scream.

As soon as I am in his sights, he thunders, "Atlas! I promise you I am going to fuck you up if you don't put my wife down."

"This wife?" I ask him innocently as I throw Savvy over my shoulder fireman style and begin backing away.

"I am going to kick your ass when I finally get down," she shrieks.

I reach over her plate and steal a piece of bacon as I keep some distance between me and Joshua. All the other brothers get out of the way as Joshua charges me, and I take off running with Savannah bouncing on my shoulder.

"I got twenty on Atlas," Jabarri says.

"I got fifty on Josh," Anson says.

"I got one hundred on Savvy," Joseph says.

We are running around the island until Savvy suddenly says, "I think I'm gonna be sick."

I stop running immediately and stand her on her feet. "I'm sorry, Savvy. Are you okay?" I ask her.

She leans over the island, and I move closer to see if I can help her. Before I can register what she is doing, she grabs the pitcher of ice water and dumps it over my head, then runs behind Josh, laughing her ass off.

This is one reason why I love my sister-in-law. From the moment she met me, she did not look at me with pity or horror. As if on cue, parts of my face begin to prickle. She doesn't care that I am an ornery bastard. She showed me the same love she did the rest of her new brothers.

It's not that I cannot form attachments with others or be in a relationship; I choose not to. When I look over at her with her arms around my brother, laughing and wiping tears from her eyes while the rest of my brothers laugh at me, a strong desire surges through me for a wife and mate too. I shake that shit off 'cause there is no woman who can love my mean ass, plus I still have a promise to fulfill. It has taken me longer than I anticipated to fulfill my promise, but I do not care if it takes me to the last day I draw breath on this earth. I will see it to completion.

Joshua took Savvy to the table, sat her in his lap, and started feeding her breakfast. Asher hands me a towel, and I dry off as best I can as I ask my brothers, "What do we need to complete today?" I begin to load up my plate. Jaasiel has made bacon, sausage, country ham, eggs, pancakes, shrimp and grits, biscuits, hash browns, tea, coffee, juice, and water.

We own our own real estate, construction company, and architectural firm. We wanted it to be a one-stop shop for buyers. We also have been toying with the idea of having our own in-house financing as well. Today we are going to get some work done on a few houses. The houses we are building for this project have all been sold, and we are ready to break ground on phase two. The last houses have finally had the rough plumbing and electrical HVAC installed. So today, we are going in to complete the drywall and interior fixtures.

Once we have that completed, the exterior house finishing team will get started. Then, we'll return to install hard surface flooring and countertops, complete exterior grading, install mirrors and shower doors, and exterior landscaping. Then a building-code official completes the final inspection and issues a certificate of occupancy. And lastly, we will perform a final walk-through.

"Then, we're going to tackle the Stephens, Clayton, and the Matthews house," Joseph says. "So it's going to be a full day."

"Are you coming with us today, Savvy?" Anson asks.

"Nope, you boys are going to have to get along without me today. I have some writing to do," she answers. She released her first book a few months ago and is in the process of writing her second one. We cleaned up the kitchen, and since there was no food to put away, we loaded the dishwasher and cleaned the counters and floors, before going to our respective cars to head to the construction site.

Atlas

I put the last nail in the drywall when my phone rings. I take my phone out and look at the screen and see that it's Doone, my contact at the D.E.A. "What's up, Doone?"

"We got a lead on another one. It's the same M.O. as all the others."

"Where?" I ask.

"I just texted you the address along with the pictures."

"Thanks, Doone," I say and hang up the phone.

Doone and I worked together at the Drug Enforcement Agency, aka D.E.A., after I left the service with an honorable discharge. I gave twenty years to the Navy as a Navy Seal on Seal Team Six, the most elite Seal team in the Navy. I finally quit the D.E.A. and came over to work for the family business. Everything I have done since I was ten years old has been to fulfill the promise I made the night my world changed. The night that still haunts me to this day.

"Is everything okay?" Aryan asked.

"Yeah, I just got to run an errand when we get done here."

He just looks at me for a second, then turns and walks off. I know I am no longer keeping my extracurricular activities hidden as well as I used to, but I refuse to let them know what I have going on. I will not lose my brothers as I make good on my promise. So if they are hurt by my excluding them, I don't care. I'd rather have them mad at me than dead.

We move on to the next house until the sun has gone down before working under the lights set up for night work. Savvy had lunch delivered to the site for us, but we worked that off almost immediately, and now I'm hungry as a savage. We order food for delivery and head home.

Everyone goes to their wing of the house when we get home to shower and change before we eat dinner. Dinner is a lively event, as usual, with all of us around the table talking shit and just enjoying being together. It wasn't always this way.

My brothers and I had a long hard road, but we got through it, and I will always be grateful, especially to Joshua. The way he held all of us together and gave his love and support is what got me through the trauma, depression, suicidal thoughts, and attempts, but mostly through my rage. He reached me when no one else could.

I look up and see Savvy watching me, and I drop my eyes back to the table before she can read anything in them. It seems like Savannah has adopted Joshua's talent for knowing when I am trying to hide shit. We finish eating, clean up the kitchen and head off to unwind.

I head back to my rooms and bide my time. While I'm waiting, I go to my hidden closet and put my code in the door. When it slides open, it reveals my collection of guns hanging neatly on the walls.

I'm good with guns, but I am better with knives. I grab my matching

HK45s, 479 Karambit, and my Glock perfection blade before heading out to the address Doone gave me. Hours later, I drag myself back into the house without running into any of my brothers. I close my bedroom door and start to pull off my shirt. I spin around when I hear Joshua's voice. He's the only person who can sneak up on me.

"Where have you been, Atlas?" he asks.

"Nowhere," I reply as I peel the shirt off my body and place it in a bag, making a mental note to burn this whole outfit later.

"You may be able to lie and hide from our other brothers, but not me. I know you've been hunting for years. You've kept it well hidden from everyone but me. But now you're not hiding it as well as you used to."

I just turn and look at him. I am not ready to have this conversation with Joshua or anyone else, so I don't say anything. He takes a deep breath as he stands to his feet.

"I have been waiting for you to let me help you with this, but I can see you are not ready yet. Just promise me one thing," he says.

"What's that?" I ask warily.

"That before you get in over your head, you come to me and let me help you."

Had he asked me this two years ago I would've made that promise, but not now–not after he found Savvy. So instead of making a promise I know I won't keep, I turn around, walk into my bathroom and close the door on any further conversation.

I hear him come closer to the door and say, "This conversation is not over." A few seconds later, I hear my bedroom door close. I finish stripping and step into the shower to wash all the grime and blood off. As I stand under the spray of water, I think about how much closer I am to my ultimate goal. Every time I catch one, they give up another one, and eventually, I am going to get to who I really want. Feeling my Glock perfection blade hit bone was very gratifying–just knowing another one of the people who destroyed my whole world was gone.

My mind reflected on this evening's kill. I wish I could've taken more time with him, but appearances must be kept. I left no trace of me or of him. Ten years as a Navy Seal has taught me how to move without a trace. *That's why they'll never see me coming.*

CHAPTER TWO

*A*tlas

I grab my bag and head to my car. My destination is about twenty hours away. Flying would be ideal, but I do not want a record of me going there. As it is, I will be taking all back roads to avoid cameras, despite the fact that the plates are cloned. The real owner of the plates is about 90 years old and lives in an assisted living facility. I'd love to see them try to pin anything on him. I get in the car, put my baseball cap and shades on, and head toward my destination. I left my main phone at home because I know Jabarri can trace it, but I have my calls forwarded to my secure phone, which is untraceable and untrackable. I have a tight timetable to get there, get the information I need, and get back here, so there will be no sleep.

I finally have the name I have spent the last thirty years trying to get. I am exhausted, but it was worth the forty-hour drive there and back. He really thought trying to reach me through my humanity was gonna work. Did he really think I would care that he was a grandfather? My parents will never get the chance to be grandparents. I gutted his ass just like his bitch ass deserved, but before he died, he whispered the name of the man who I truly wanted. As soon as I get home, I'll try to find everything I can on Victor Sanchez.

I take the truck to the chop shop to be broken into pieces, destroyed, or sold, and walk a couple of blocks over to my car to drive home. I head directly to my room to shower. I changed clothes and burned them in the garage, but I needed a long hot shower to clear my head of everything I had to do these past couple of days.

I look in the mirror at the scar that runs across my entire face, and I can still feel the blade as it splits my face open. I wasn't expected to live, but I did out of sheer hate and determination. I shower until the water turns cold and still stand there, waiting, but I don't know what for. Eventually, I turn the water off and get out. I towel dry my hair, wrap a towel around my waist, and sit at my desk. Opening my laptop, I type in the name Victor Sanchez. He is a real estate company owner, of all things. He isn't married, and has no kids listed. He has a mansion…*Wait, am I reading this right? He's in Texas? This whole time he's been two states over?* I want to be angry by this revelation, but how can I? I could have walked right past him, and I wouldn't have known.

All I remember was the fear in their voices when they talked about him. Even at that age, I knew he was the boss, the one calling the shots. It has taken years to finally get high enough to get his name, and now not only do I have his name, I have a picture and his address. He's an average-looking…black man? I look again at the picture. No, he's not just black. He is definitely mixed with another race but I cannot pinpoint what that may be.

After all these years, I am finally going to finish this. I am going to fulfill the promise I made to my father. But this has to be planned just right. It has to be a surgical strike. Get in, kill him, and get back out without a trace. I need to take my time, research, do some reconnaissance, and when I feel the time is right….strike. Every instinct I have is telling me to go to Texas right now and kill his ass, but I'd probably get killed trying something so reckless. He is undoubtedly very protected. Well, I know what I'll be doing the next few weekends. I grab my go-kit and pull out an ID and the credit card that goes with the name so that I can find a place to rent while I am getting intel on Victor. I continue researching this bastard until I hear a knock on the door.

"Yeah!" I yell.

The door opens, and in walks my favorite person, Savvy.

"Hey, sis," I say to her.

"You didn't come down for dinner, and I wanted to make sure you were okay," she says as she strolls further into the room.

Looking out the window and seeing the sun has risen and set lets me know I've been sitting in front of my computer for hours. Putting the computer in sleep mode, I go into my walk-in closet, grab some black sweatpants and a t-shirt and put them on. I come out to see she has brought me dinner.

"Sit down and keep me company," I tell her.

She sits down on the sofa next to me as I begin eating the meal.

"What's going on, Atlas?"

"What do you mean, Savvy?" I ask like I don't know what she's talking about.

"Don't do that, Atlas. I thought we were closer than that." Savvy says with hurt in her eyes.

"We are, Savannah, but you are not going to have Joshua coming after me. There is only one man I know for sure who can beat me, and that is your husband."

She just sits there looking at me, "I love you," she says softly.

"I love you too."

"Please ask for help when the time comes."

"I will not make that promise, Savvy. I wouldn't know what to do if something were to happen to one of my brothers because of what I'm into," I tell her.

"Atlas, your brothers would bring an ice storm to hell if you needed them to," she reminds me.

"I know that," I say.

"Well at least promise me you will keep the option open, please."

"For you, I will, Savvy."

She stands to take my plate, and I pull her into a hug. Of course, right at that moment, Josh walks in. "Atlas, get your hands off my, you fucker."

Stubbornly, I pull Savannah even closer, "She doesn't seem to want to let go of me," I say mockingly.

"Stop it, Atlas," Savvy laughs as she wiggles out of my arms and goes into Josh's arms. Then she grabs my plate and walks out of the room.

"Don't break her heart, Atlas," he says, walking away after his wife. I go to bed with my plan firmly in place.

CHAPTER THREE

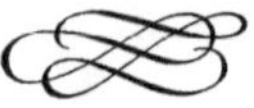

wo Months Later...

I wake up slowly. I have had the same dream every night since arriving here in Texas. Being here, watching Victor, and planning his death has definitely brought my memories to the forefront. I have been watching Victor waiting for the right time to strike. Tonight it's time to make my move. This son of a bitch is a piece of work. I have watched him parade a stream of barely, if legal, girls in and out of his mansion.

Most of them leave looking like they have gone three rounds with a heavy-weight boxer. If not that, they're passed around to his guards. I cannot wait to kill this motherfucker and as many of his guards as I can, fucking pedophiles. I am tracking where they are getting these girls from so I can shut that shit down too. Victor is only in his fifties but still old enough to be these girls' grandfather. I wonder what he would do if his own daughter were treated like he treats these teenage girls. But according to his records, he has no daughters, or sons for that matter, which is unusual considering all the girls and women he goes through. Maybe he got a vasectomy, or perhaps he's sterile. Either way, I am glad another person isn't running around with his DNA.

I grab my gear, dismantle my HK45C compact and put the pieces on me to reassemble once I'm inside Victor's mansion. On nights like this, the guards will be light, and the drinking will be plentiful. They usually make sure to bring enough girls in for the guards too. I befriended one of the guys, named Frank, whose job was to bring the girls to the mansion. I was surprised to catch him trying to free the girls not long after they pulled up, but seeing some guards coming his way, I managed to distract them so they wouldn't get caught. Later, he admitted to me that he took the job, not knowing all that it entailed because he needed the money.

"I should have known it was too good to be true," Frank tells me.

"That much money just to deliver a package? I never dreamed the package would be girls, but my wife and I are expecting our seventh child and need a bigger place. I needed money and fast. The baby will be here soon."

I got Frank to introduce me as another guy in desperate need of money in exchange for a fully paid six-bedroom house in a part of Texas far away from here. I was guaranteed to get in since he is the ring leader's cousin. After tonight, Frank and his wife and children will be far away from here. Victor will be dead, these girls will be safe, and I will finally have fulfilled my promise. All in a night's work.

I meet Frank at the safe house where they are keeping the girls. We load them up and head for the mansion. When I got there, I put my weapons bag underneath the spare tire, and patted my jacket where the pieces of my HK were hidden on me. As we ride to Victor's, I center myself and prepare to finally fulfill the promise I made thirty years ago.

We finally arrive and are let through the gates with the minimal search I was counting on. We park in front of the house. The front door opens, and another six guards pour out to the truck. They don't search us again but begin to pick out the girls they want for themselves.

There are two girls who I do not think are legal. They look barely 16 years old. *He definitely has a type.* They look like they could be sisters, they are both dark-skinned black girls, but they look more

Afro-Latina with long wavy black hair and cognac brown eyes, and both are on the thick side. They will be beautiful women once they're older, and I will make sure they get that chance. They remind me of my niece, Skai, the little spitfire she is. If anyone ever dared take her, they'd have to kill her. That little walking disaster will not go down without a fight. She is one hundred percent Savvy's daughter, with attitude and brains to match.

They take those girls in the back to Victor's bedroom while we stay in the open floor plan-designed living room and kitchen area. The music is booming, and the alcohol is flowing. There are about seven guards with around fifteen girls. Some of these girls have been here before and know the routine, but there are a few who look terrified and have huddled together in a corner to try to make themselves invisible.

I go over to the bar where they have the alcohol, and I slip in a drug that should have them knocked out in less than ten minutes. As I wait for the drugs to take effect so I can slip down the hall to Victor's bedroom, I slip out to the truck and retrieve my other weapons. Once I have the weapons secured to my body, I walk back in to discover all the guards have finally passed out. I tell the girls that are in the room to stay here and be quiet. It was easy for them to listen; I looked mean as hell and a bit scary with my scar. I head towards the bedroom, but when I get there, I see the other guard walking into

Victor's room taking off his shirt, heading towards the bed where the two girls are. They have the sheets pulled up to their necks, eyes wide, watching the guard move towards them.

I pull out my HK45 compact, screw on the suppressor, and put a bullet in the back of his kneecap. He falls forward on the bed, screaming and holding his knee. I put the barrel right between his eyes and tell him to shut up before I put a bullet in the other knee. "Where is Victor!?"

"I don't know," he cries.

I aim the gun at the other knee, and he yells that Victor got a call and left. I want to roar. I was so close, and I missed him. I take the butt of the gun and hit him across the temple, and knock him out. I tell the girls to get dressed and come with me, and they scramble out of the bed and grab their clothes. As they are getting dressed, they keep trying not to look at my face. We leave the bedroom, and I check every door on my way back towards the living room. Some of the guards left with girls to various bedrooms, and since no one came running when the guard screamed, either they were too busy or knocked out too.

I open the doors and either tell the girl I find there to get dressed and come on out or put a bullet in the guard's head and tell the girl to get dressed. I opened one of the doors, but the scene on the other side was completely different from the others. A woman is tied to a bed, and she is definitely not a girl. All she has on is her bra and panties. She is bruised on every inch of her body, from her feet to her head.

Her face is so severely beaten that one of her eyes is swollen shut, and her face is misshapen from the beating she's been subjected to. She must have been here for days. She is lying in her own excrement and urine. I take my knife out and cut her from the bed. I go back to another room and grab one of the cleaner sheets and blanket to wrap her up in. When I go to lift her, she puts up a feeble fight.

"Stop!" I say to her, "I'm not going to hurt you. I'm going to get you out of here." I lift her into my arms and head out the door.

In the end, I killed all of the guards and the traffickers, and Frank's cousin. I rescued all fifteen of the girls and this woman in my arms. We head out the side door of the mansion and cut through the grass to the back of the estate. We climbed through a hole I cut in the fence and got in the SUV I left there.

We pile into the car and head towards my house. Once we're there, I grab bread and deli meats, condiments, and drinks from the refrigerator for the girls to eat. Soon after, we put sheets and comforters over the sofas in the living room. Some girls collapse there, and others go into the spare bedrooms. I carry the woman in one of the spare bedrooms next to mine and call Doone to tell him about the girls. He tells me he will be here in the morning. After hanging up, I get a glass of water and some soup for the woman. When I enter the bedroom, she has not moved from where I left her. I set the bowl and glass of water on the nightstand and walk into the adjoining bathroom. Wetting a facecloth, I come back into the bedroom, sit on the side of the bed, and wipe her face. She needs to go to a hospital, but I instinctively know that I shouldn't take her there.

She begins to stir and then opens her eyes–well, the one that isn't swollen, and my breath catches in my throat because they are the most beautiful cognac brown. She looks like an older version of the two girls brought in for Victor. Who is she? I wonder as I finish washing her face as best I can. "Are you hungry?"

She barely nods her head, but the message is clear. She tries to prop herself up, but she doesn't have the strength to sit herself up. I put my hands under her arms and gently pull her up to prop her against some pillows. I begin to spoon-feed her the soup. She is obviously hungry, and I wondered when was the last time she ate, and glancing at the bruised ruts on her wrist, I wondered how long she'd been tied to that bed.

Before long, the soup and water are gone. "Are you able to get up?" I ask her. "I thought you might want to take a shower or use the bathroom."

"I want to take a shower, but I do not think I can do it on my own," she tells me.

"I'll see if one of the older girls can help you," I suggest.

"Can you help me?" she pleaded.

"Excuse me?"

"I want you to help me. I trust you. Please," she asks.

I just stare at her because she looks at me like I don't have a scar across my face or as if she didn't witness me kill a bunch of people tonight. "Um, okay," I say. I'm at a complete loss for any other words.

I walk into my bedroom and grab one of my t-shirts. I walk back into the room and go straight to the bathroom. I turn the shower on, then go to the room, lift her out of the bed, and carry her to the bathroom. Lowering her to the teak bench just outside the shower stall, I strip down to my boxer briefs while she takes off her bra and panties. When she's ready, I help her stand and slip my arm beneath hers, allowing her to lean on me as we walk into the shower stall. She leans against me as the heated water runs down her body. My eyes roam over the purplish bruises covering her body. She has been severely beaten. "Can you breathe?"

"Yes, it just hurts," she says softly.

I gently press my fingers against her ribcage, and she hisses in pain. "You probably have some broken ribs. I should take you to the hospital."

"No, please. No hospital."

"You can't be alone in this condition."

"I'll be okay. I can take care of myself."

"I know you just met me, but do you trust me?" I ask her.

"Yes," she answers almost immediately. "I don't know why, but I do."

"Good, then I'll take care of it."

"What does that mean?" she asks.

"I got you, is what it means." I gently use the loofah to wash her with Nivea lavender body wash and wash and condition her hair with the same products Savvy uses. I once used her products when I ran out of my own, and I loved them so much that I began to purchase them for myself. Once her hair and body were clean, I turned the water off, grabbed a towel, and began to dry her off. By the time I dry myself off, she is damn near asleep standing up. I wrap the towel around my waist and a towel sheet around her and carry her to my bedroom. I lay her in my bed, and she is asleep before I can pull the blanket over her.

In the other bedroom, I strip the bed, grab her underthings, and put them in the washing machine. While they are washing, I check on the other girls to ensure they are okay. I put fresh sheets on the bed and cleaned up the bathroom. Once that was done, a few girls came in to sleep. I put the clothes in the dryer, go back to my bedroom, get in bed as far away from her as possible, and go to sleep.

CHAPTER FOUR

Atlas

I wake up with a start, feeling like something is off, but I can't quite put a finger on what it is. I look over to my right and see that the mystery woman is still asleep, and that's when it hits me. I didn't have the dream. I head to the bathroom to take care of my morning needs. Once done, I flush, wash my hands, brush my teeth, and wash my face.

That done, I take a proper shower. I don't take long, and I hurry to get out. I dry off, moisturize so I'm not ashy as Savvy says, and throw on some boxer briefs, jeans, a t-shirt, and boots. As I lace up my boots, I hear a small voice coming from the bedroom and go out to see what's wrong.

"Can you help me to the bathroom, please?" the mystery woman asks. *I really need to ask her what her name is.*

"Sure," I say, grabbing a t-shirt off the foot of the bed and help her put it on, and carrying her to the toilet.

"I can manage," she insists once she's seated. "I'll call you when I'm ready."

"Okay," I say and start to head out of the bathroom. Once I get to the door, I stop, and without turning around, I ask, "By the way, what is your name?"

"True. What's yours?"

"Nice to meet you, True. I'm Atlas," I say and walk out. I head to the dryer and pull out the linens and her bra and panties. I place an order with a local diner and pay extra for delivery. Once that is done, I head back into my room and ask True if she is ready to which she answers the affirmative. I help her up and stand with her as she washes her hands, brushes her teeth, and washes her face. I put leave-in conditioner in her hair last night, so I did her hair in three braids. I walk with her to the bed, where she sees her underwear. I leave to give her some privacy to put them on when I hear the doorbell.

The girls have scattered, and if I didn't know better, I wouldn't believe anyone was here other than me. I open the door, and it's the food. I take the food and give the delivery guy a generous tip.

Taking the food to the dining room table, I unpack it, and the girls filter back in. I make True a plate and a glass of orange juice and take it to her. I ask about her clothing and shoe size and leave her to eat in peace. Next, I go to the dining room and get the same information from all the girls there. That done, I told them not to leave or answer the door and that I would be back shortly.

I climb in my truck and head up the street to a clothing store where I simplify things by picking up sweatpants, t-shirts, sneakers, and basic underwear. I skipped getting bras, but I did get those tank tops with built-in bras and some other basic essentials. After that, I pay for everything and head back to the house. Once there, I give the girls the bags and let them work out who gets what. I take True's bag to her in the bedroom to find her asleep. I lay the clothes on the bed for her, walk out of the room, and go to my temporary office. A couple of hours later, Doone is at the door.

"Jesus, Atlas! What did you do?" Doone asks as he sees the fifteen girls I rescued.

"I got these girls out of being sex trafficked. Some of them have homes to go back to. Most either don't or won't go back to their families since it was their family that sold them into the sex slave trade. Can you help them?" I ask Doone.

"Yeah, let me make a few calls," Doone says.

Several hours later, I watched the last of the girls leave with Doone. He called in a few favors and got some of the girls who were in really bad situations new identities. I helped to secure finances and housing. Hopefully, this will be a fresh start for them. I put some latex gloves on and began cleaning every inch of the apartment, wiping, vacuuming, and disinfecting everything. Then, I made a bowl of soup, a small sandwich, and some Gatorade to replenish her electrolytes and brought it all to True. When I got to the bedroom, she was dressed in the clothes I bought for her and was sitting on the side of the bed. Although she looks stronger, she still looks like she's been through hell.

"Is it time to go?" she asks.

"Yes."

She stands up while favoring her left side and slowly walks to me. I walk her out to the truck. I've bagged all the linens and sprayed all the surfaces with a hydrogen peroxide mixture. If anyone does find the apartment, there won't be any DNA or fingerprints to lead back to me, True, or any of the girls.

I throw the bags of linen in the back of the SUV and head towards home. Halfway there, I put True in a hotel room while I take this SUV to a chop shop, burn the linens in a ten-gallon steel drum, and get in the other SUV I left parked nearby. I swing back by the hotel, pick True up, and then continue home. I only stop long enough to grab food, a pillow, and a blanket for True and push it home using the back roads.

Finally, after driving for almost seventeen hours, I'm home–my home–not the compound. No one knows I own this house. It's in my paternal grandmother's maiden name. I park the SUV in the garage and go around to help True out. I carry her in the house to the spare bedroom across the hall from my room, lay her on the bed, take her shoes off, and cover her with the comforter. I go across the hall to my room. I sit on the bed and hold my head in my hands. *What the hell did I do?*

Victor

I walk through my house only to see all my guards are dead, and the girls are gone, including True. When Roman called me and told me he found everyone dead, I came home asap to find this shit. I found the guard in my bed, and above the bed, written in blood, were the words *"**Next time, Mother Fucker!!!**"* No one has ever gotten this close to me. Had I never gotten the call that forced me to leave, that would have been me dead in my bed. I have gotten too lax in my personal security. Obviously, that has to change. I want to put a bullet in every guard here, but it's not their fault. They weren't even there.

I scratch the side of my head with the barrel of the gun I don't remember pulling out. I have been careful in my dealings over the years, not letting anyone I have had a problem with live. I made sure not to have children so they could not be used against me as leverage. But someone must have slipped through the cracks, and I have no idea who it could have been.

It has taken me over thirty years to build my empire. When I got into this game, I was young and broke, but I was smart and ambitious. During those early years, when I was trying to make a name for myself, I made a lot of mistakes. I moved up the ladder and became invaluable to the head of the cartel. I watched him and learned everything I could, including the routes and contacts.

Once I learned everything I could, I created a shadow cartel right up under Carlos's nose. Every move he made, I made a matching one, and before he knew what hit him, I had completely taken over and destroyed his organization. I killed him, his wife and children, and every loyal soldier he had. I learned to use pressure points to make moves to expand my business out of Columbia into the southwest of America. It took more work than I initially thought it would, but I eventually found a way to expand in the United States, and now I pretty much run the entire southwest region. It was during this time I was the most sloppy in my dealings. I hadn't learned not to leave witnesses or people who might want vengeance alive. I was also working with a bunch of idiots who fucked up so many deals. It's a wonder I was able to kill Carlos and take over his organization. I put them on low-level work like managing my smaller businesses, things I didn't care about if they fucked them up. But now someone got close to me. Not just close to me, but in my house, and I have no idea who it could be.

I picked up the guard's dead foot and throw it off my thousand-dollar bedding before taking a seat. I called a cleaning crew in to get out the bodies and clean up the mess then made plans to go to my compound near Buenaventura until I could get this under control. I checked the video feed, but someone wiped the supposedly unhack-able security system, so I have no idea who was here. Anyone who did see who did this is dead. I called the guy who supplied the girls, but he answered and told me not to call him anymore. He found his guys dead, too. All the girls were gone, and his video feed was wiped clean too.

"Eduardo!" I bark into the phone, "Get off your lazy ass and get the jet ready. I need to be in Buenaventura as soon as possible."

Eduardo handles my travel but has become a lazy, fat, complacent waste of space. Maybe I'll kill him and let someone else take his job; he's damn near useless. Could it be something connected with True? I should have just killed her, but she had to learn a lesson, and now she's gone too. She's a loose end I should have ended years ago, but I thought maybe one day she could be useful. Now I regret that decision. Over the years, she has mostly been on the periphery of my life and not quite important enough to change that.

The sound of the barrel of a gun dragging along the hallway wall is like nails on a chalkboard to my ears as I make my way to the room I was holding her in. I lean against the door jamb and look at the bed where she'd been tied as if I can make her reappear. *Is she dead? Will she come back? Is this her doing? Is it even connected?*

Until I get answers, I will go away. My second in command will remain here to investigate and get answers. If he fails, I will flay him alive and kill his entire family–children and parents. Max walks up to me, and before he can open his mouth, I turn and shoot him in the head. If I can't kill who I want to, he can serve as a proxy. I feel a little better as I walk back out of my house, get in the car, and head to the airstrip.

CHAPTER FIVE

True

I wake up in another strange bed. Seconds later, all the memories come crashing back, and I wonder if I made a mistake trusting Atlas. He is one scary-looking son of a bitch, with that scar running across his face. But I feel safe with him, and that's not something I say easily. I have felt like I was on the outside looking in at my whole life, never really feeling like I belong. Surprisingly, in the small amount of time I have spent with Atlas, I feel a belonging deep in my bones–not just me belonging to him–but him belonging to me. I hold my head as I get up to go find the bathroom. I must have taken too many hits on the head during the beating Victor gave me. My head is spinning. Just as I sit up in the bed, there is a knock on the door.

"True?" I recognize the deep, male voice as Atlas'.

"Yeah?" I responded.

"Can I come in?" he asks.

"Um, yeah, I guess," I say. The door swings open in a near-silent swoosh.

"Is there anything I can get for you?" he asks me.

"Yeah, can you help me to the bathroom?" I ask.

"Sure," he says as he comes over to the bed and helps me up, and we take a short walk to the bathroom. He makes sure I am good before he leaves me to handle my business. I slowly make it to the sink to wash my hands, and just as I feel like my legs might give out, Atlas is there to carry me not to the bed I woke up in but to the bed across the hall in what I assume is his bedroom.

"I'd like to call a doctor to look you over; if you're okay with that? Off the books," he adds.

"Yes, I'm okay with that," I say, and Atlas takes his phone out and calls someone named Doone.

"Someone will be here within the hour," he says as he hangs up the phone.

An hour later, I had been poked and prodded to the point of screaming. I have lacerations, puncture wounds, a few broken ribs, a couple of broken fingers that got reset and taped, and an orbital floor fracture. If Atlas hadn't come that night and rescued me, I would have laid in that room and died.

The doctor talked to Atlas in hushed tones that I couldn't hear, then handed him a couple of pill bottles and left after promising he'd be back in a couple of days to check my progress.

"I'd like you to stay in my room so I can keep a better eye on you," says Atlas.

I turn to look at Atlas. "Where are you going to sleep?" I ask because I hope he doesn't think he's going to sleep in the bed with me, even if it is his bed. However, this bed is the largest bed I have ever seen. He could get in while I lay sideways, and I still wouldn't be able to touch him.

"I'll sleep on the sofa."

I take a look at what he calls a sofa, and it's wide enough to be a full-sized bed and long enough for a baby giant. "Will you be comfortable?"

"Yes, I made sure. I had furniture custom-made large enough for my generous size," he smiles.

I nod my head and lay back on the bed, exhausted.

. . .

Atlas

I look at the woman, the only woman ever to lay or sleep in my bed. She is so little compared to me. She looks like a toddler instead of a grown woman. I have an Alberta King-sized bed, one of the biggest beds you can get. My brothers and I have either the Alberta King or Texas King-sized bed. But of course, once Josh got married he upgraded to the Alaskan King-sized bed and has been talking about getting the family size or family XL. I do not know why I can't imagine him letting Savannah sleep anywhere away from him.

I turn the tv on and make sure the volume is low so as not to disturb True while I plot. I want to ask True why she was in Victor's house and beaten within an inch of her life, but I will wait until she is better. I hope I did not make a mistake by bringing her here, but after the doctor came and examined her, I know without a doubt she would have died if she stayed in that house any longer.

She was malnourished and dehydrated on top of the physical injuries she suffered. The doctor left antibiotics and pain pills. She took the antibiotics but adamantly refused to take the pain pills the doctor left or anything for her. Once she took the pills, she ate again and fell asleep before I could put the dishes on the nightstand.

I go over to my computer and pull up the security feed from Victor's compound. A few taps later, I watch Victor walk into his house and discover the dead bodies and the girls missing. I read his lips as he made a call ordering his plane to be readied to take him to Columbia. *Fucking Columbia!* Could I follow him? Yes. Will I follow him? No. So until he brings his bitch ass back to America, I will regroup and plan. I plan on dismantling his real-estate company and his organization. Doone will get the credit, but I will get the reward. So let the games begin. I shut the computer back down and then go over to the sofa, lie down, and go to sleep while keeping True safe.

True

I wake up the next morning and wish I had taken a pain pill but knowing what drugs did to my mother caused me to never want to touch them, no matter the circumstances. I look over, expecting to see Atlas sleeping on the bed he calls a sofa, and he's not there. Damn, now I have to get to the bathroom myself. This shit is tricky with one good eye; my peripheral and depth perception sucks. Just as I go to throw the cover back, the door swings open and vibrates as it rebounds from the force of Atlas's entrance.

"Oh, sorry," he says. "I didn't realize how hard I pushed the door open."

"I can see that. I'm glad I wasn't asleep. You would've scared the hell out of me."

A wince crossed his face as he said, "Yeah, sorry."

I finally notice he's carrying a tray in both hands that's overflowing with food. I look from the tray to him, wondering who he thinks can eat all of that. Then I remember he's huge, so…yeah, probably him. He puts the tray on the coffee table. "Do you need to go to the bathroom?" he asks.

"Oh, um, yes," I forgot that I had to pee. I was so busy watching the veins bulge in his arms as he carried the tray. He comes over and picks me up off the bed, and walks me into the ensuite.

"I can walk, Atlas," I tell him.

"And I can carry you, True," he responds. He stands me on my feet but holds on to make sure I'm steady. Once he's sure I'm good, he walks out of the water closet. The door quietly clicks closed behind him. I sit down, and while nature is doing what she does, I'm thinking. I cannot go back home. I have no home to go to. After Victor caught me, he killed my parents, and I do not have any brothers or sisters, but I did have an escape plan if I succeeded in killing Victor. Maybe I'll follow the plan I had until I can come up with something better. I finish up, flush and head over to the sink to wash my hands.

As soon as I turn the water on, the bathroom door swings open, and Atlas is there. He goes straight to the shower and turns it on, walks into the closet, and grabs a towel, shower cap, body wash, and body scrub. He comes over to me and begins to strip me out of my clothes like I am a toddler. When he has me naked, he strips himself to his boxer briefs, picks me up, and walks into the shower. He sets me on the shower bench, and gets to work. After that, he washes and scrubs damn near every inch of my body except where I want him to touch most. Since I am just about eye level with him and those boxer briefs ain't hiding much, I know he isn't unaffected either.

He hands me a washcloth and the body wash and flees the shower. If I even graze this washcloth across my pussy I will cum. I have to sit for a full ten minutes or more so my body can calm all the way down, and I wash as fast as I can and call for Atlas to help me out. He comes back in, swaddles me in a bath sheet, and carries me out to the bed. When he grabs the bottle of lotion, I move so fast to snatch it out of his hands I wince in pain.

"I can lotion myself, Atlas," I say breathlessly. There is no way in hell I can go through that sensual torture again and not beg him to fuck me, damn my injuries. He eyes me for a second and then leaves me to go back in the bathroom to most likely take his own shower.

Once he is gone, I slap the lotion on as fast as I can but then quickly realize I have nothing to wear. I rewrap myself in the bath sheet and hobble over to the sofa and begin eating from the platter he brought in earlier. Even though the food is barely warm, it is still delicious. As I'm stuffing my mouth with my fourth piece of bacon, Atlas walks back in with a towel hanging low on his hips, carrying shopping bags.

"I brought you some clothes," Atlas says.

"Thank you," I say.

"No problem. I'll let you get dressed," he says and heads back into the bathroom.

I hurry up and dress while Atlas is still in the bathroom, and I am lying on the sofa exhausted by the time he comes out dressed. A t-shirt and gray sweatpants, really gray sweatpants. He might as well have kept on the boxer briefs. He's a tease, I decide, and here I am, looking like I got beat with an ugly stick. Well, I did get beat, so, oh never mind, I think, as I find myself on an irrational tangent. He brings me two antibiotics to take, and I swallow them diligently, and before I can even register it happening, I'm falling back to sleep.

Atlas

Two weeks of this, and I'm looking online to see if ball slings exist. Every day of washing her and holding her next to my body has given me the worst case of blue balls in the history of blue balls. I don't even want a warm tropical breeze to skitter across my ball hairs let alone the skin of my balls. I chant like it's a prayer that she's hurt, so I can't take her like my body is craving. My dick and balls have given me an eviction notice cause they're over it. And it is literally nothing she is doing. Hell, all she can do is eat, use the bathroom, and sleep, as her body is healing.

I have never been so attracted to a woman in all my life. The more her body heals, and the bruises fade, the more her beauty comes through, and the more I want her.

I gave her a phone that I call every day to make sure she takes the antibiotics, eats, and gets to the bathroom when I am working, and that allows me to rest easy when I am away from home. She is quickly becoming important to me, and that frightens me a little. I have never thought about having a woman in my life.

Oh, I have no problems getting women to fuck me, but that is as far as I want it to go. Women like the thrill of sleeping with me and perhaps the money, but not one of them has ever made me want to let them know me beyond getting my nut off. True, however, called to me even when she was a mess in the bed where I found her, and I am not sure how I feel about that. It's more than just a physical attraction, however. It is the strength she has shown, her utter determination to get better. To live and not die. But there are other times when she is vulnerable, and I'm cocky enough to think she does not show anyone that side of her. The day I walked into the room and she was lying in bed weeping made me want to fly to Columbia and pull Victor's spinal column from his body through his throat. I gathered her in my arms, and she held onto me and cried. That was the first time I caught her like this, but it was not the last. I have found her sitting in the corner of the shower damn near hysterical. I sat down on the floor fully dressed, pulled her in my arms, and let her get it all out.

The trauma even seeps into her dreams. She didn't have night-mares like me, but she would cry and beg in her sleep. I would go to her in the bed and hold her and let her know she was safe. And it is not a one-way street. I woke from a nightmare with True caressing my face and offering me comfort. Two broken people taking the broken pieces of their hearts to make the other's heart whole. No, I will not let her go, and I don't care who I have to fight to keep her, including her. No matter the thoughts and insecurities floating around in my head, I am still drawn to her. But I have not just been lusting after my roommate these past two weeks.

I have been quietly buying up businesses that Victor owns. The low-hanging fruit that he has neglected while he was walking around being a failed abortion. Businesses that he has left men in charge of those who have pressure points, usually money problems who are happy to give up these businesses for the right price and no questions. He is a sorry excuse for a man, let alone a human. His momma shouldn't have swallowed him; she should have spit his ass in the toilet where he belongs. A couple of used car dealerships, laundromats, strip clubs, and bodegas, once his, are all mine now. I have taken the businesses I've bought and am giving them to women who have come out of domestic violence or DV situations and want to get their lives and independence back. Once they go through the proper educational courses, they will be trained to manage them and eventually to own them free and clear.

I had my lawyer set up a foundation for survivors of sex trafficking, and they will have the same opportunity as the women in the DV program. Even once these businesses are claimed, I will work with the organizations and other businesses to help these women and survivors own and run the businesses of their choice. At least Victor's punk ass will bring some good in these lives when he has caused such misery in so many others. When he brings his punk ass back to the United States, he's not gonna have shit left to come back to.

I look over to True as she sleeps in my bed, and I wonder who she really is and why Victor had her tied to that bed and left to die. I haven't pushed her because of how hurt she is, but she is going to have to start giving up answers and soon. She hasn't asked me to let anyone know she is ok or to call anyone on her behalf. I don't think she has anyone else. I have no problem with her staying here as long as there are no ramifications. If she doesn't want to stay here, I can set her up in one of the houses we still own in one of the subdivisions, but until I can put Victor out of his misery, here is the safest place for her. *Yeah, that's bullshit; I just want her here with me.*

I'm at the family compound this morning. I left my house extra early because I felt like I hadn't spent any time with my brothers these past few weeks. As soon as I round the corner to the kitchen-family room area, I can hear them loud and talking shit. Once they see me, Asher says, "Oh, look who decided to grace us with his presence." I flip him the bird as I head straight to the refrigerator.

"Did you just come down to eat?" Jaasiel asks me.

"Yeah, I'm a growing boy," I say as I grab the platter of breakfast sandwiches Jaasiel made and the bowl of fresh fruit. I grab three sausage egg and cheese sandwiches and make a bowl of fruit and grab a bottle of water, then I pop a squat at the island and tuck in.

"So you got a chick stashed away somewhere?" Aryan asks.

I almost choked on the bite I just took. Aryan is too close to the truth.

"Oh, must be. he didn't even try to deny it," Anson says.

"You guys sit around this kitchen like some fucked up testosterone-filled version of the Golden Girls and just flap your damn gums. Ain't there some other shit you guys could be doing?"

"Nope," they all say at the same time, looking at me deadpan.

"I hate all of you," I grumble as they laugh at me.

"So, for real, who is she?" Aryan asks.

" I don't know what you're talking about," I say.

"Hmm, maybe we'll follow you so we can meet her," Jabarri says, "It should be easy to track your phone."

"I mean, you can, and when you do, be prepared for the repercussions. Since when do we get into each other's private lives?"

"When did you start sneaking around?" Asher says.

"Listen, don't get fucked up trying to be nosey. Leave the shit alone."

"I don't know what the big deal is, Atlas," Jassiel says.

"The big deal is he said to leave him the fuck alone. So, leave him the fuck alone! It's none of y'all's goddamned business," says Joseph, who is usually pretty quiet and reserved. But today, he walked in like a pissed-off bear. It's dead silence in the kitchen after that statement as we all revert back to little boys.

"Thanks, Joseph," I mumble.

He just grunts as he snatches a sandwich off the platter. Then he takes the rest of the bowl of fruit to eat by himself.

As soon as he sits at the island, Jabari asks him, "Who pissed in your Cheerios?" And once again, everything is back to normal, with everyone laughing, including Joseph.

"Fuck off, Jabarri," Joseph says, and before he can respond, the door slams open as a little menace walks in.

"Uncle Seph! Uncle Atlas!" she runs over to get swept up in bear hugs from both of us.

"What are you doing here, Skai?" Joseph asks.

"I came for a long-overdue spa day, some shopping, and some food," she says while snatching the sandwich right out of Joseph's hands and biting into it. "Hmmm," she moans, "Uncle Jaasiel, you really are a genius in the kitchen," she says around a mouthful of sandwich.

"Thank you, Skai," he says with a chuckle.

"I don't know where you put all the food you eat," Aryan says, looking at her. At five feet, one inch, and just barely one hundred and ten pounds, she was the epitome of petite; but ate like a starting linebacker.

"Right here," she says as she pats her nonexistent stomach. As she finishes the stolen sandwich, I ask her.

"Does your mother know you're here?"

"Nope. I will text her in a minute and let her know I'm out here."

"Why don't you just go back to their wing and let her know?" Anson asks.

"And what, lose an eye, Uncle Anson?" she asks. "Ain't no telling what I'm liable to find on the other side of that door. It's a no for me, love. I will send her this text and let her come on out here to me. Thank you very much."

"Well, it's pretty inconvenient to just pop up here and expect your mother to just cater to your little whims," Jabarri said.

Skai stopped what she was doing and turned her full attention to him. "And it was inconvenient that your mother missed her birth control pill and fucked up and had you, but you can't win them all."

It's well known among us that Jabarri was an oops-baby. Our mother thought she was going through menopause but was actually pregnant. So sixteen years after she had Jaasiel, she found herself pregnant with Jabarri. It's a sore spot for him, and Skai just applied pressure to it.

"You are such a brat," Jabarri spits out.

"And you are such an ass."

"Don't you have some classes you should be at?"

"Shouldn't there be a zookeeper here to keep an eye on you? I mean, after all, you just learned not to drag your knuckles on the floor."

I bite my lip to keep from laughing, and I peek over at Jabarri, who's so mad the tips of his ears are beet red. He opens his mouth, but nothing comes out, so he closes it and tries again, and he still can't form a sentence.

Skai looked at him and shook her head much as you would at a child trying to walk but just not quite getting the hang of it. She reached over and patted his hand. "It's ohh-kay," she says real slow and loud, "I'll talk in little words so you can understand. I'm sure they can add some extra lessons for you. I mean, one step at a time, right? And talking is so hard for a primate of your limited intelligence. Maybe we can get you a picture book so you can point to what you want to say." With that, she jumps off the stool and heads back to her mother's suite of rooms.

As soon as she's out of sight, we roar with laughter. "Shut up," Jabarri says, looking like the baby of the family.

"Why don't you just stop being a dick to her and ask her out," Anson says.

"First of all, Joshua, second, she has a girlfriend, and third, she is technically my niece."

"Excuses," I tell him. "Man the fuck up and talk to Josh and Savvy about your intentions if she means that much to you. As far as her being your niece, she's what, three years younger than you? And you've been her quote, unquote uncle for all of two years. Stop making excuses before someone else snatches her ass up, or she marries her girlfriend, and they have a baby with a willing donor." I tell him and walk out the kitchen.

CHAPTER SEVEN

tlas

"ATLAS, can you go to the store for me?"

"What do you need?" I had no problems grabbing anything she felt she needed. Right after I brought her here, I went to the store and picked up panties, bras, socks, nightgowns, t-shirts, and sweatpants, along with pads and Midol.

"Well, you don't have anything in this room," she states matter of factly which causes me to look around at my bedroom.

"I don't know what you mean. There's a bed, dressers, nightstands, a tv, a work desk with multiple computers, a sofa, a table, a refrigerator, and an ensuite. What more do you want?"

"Something to do," she replies. "There's nothing to occupy my time while you are gone all day, and I'm tired of watching tv."

Oh. I guess she's right. The only thing I ever needed was a bed, bathroom, and computers. "What can I get you?"

"Do you have an e-reader around here? Perhaps I can download some books, board games, and play cards? I don't know… anything."

I just blink at her, I have never had or done any of those things. If it didn't involve getting to Victor, it didn't serve a purpose in my life. "Um, I'll see what I can get for you," I say as I grab my keys and head out to dig up the stuff she's asked me for. I stop at Target, and once inside, I grab an associate about Skai's age and tell her what I'm looking for.

I walk out of the store, looking at my receipt and shaking my head. I came for three or four things, and instead, I have four bags full of stuff, and I'm over $500 poorer. *How the hell did this happen? This store is the devil.*

I grabbed at least six different games, an e-reader, and the girl made sure she opened it, set it up, and downloaded at least 20 books from various authors and I grabbed more fuzzy socks, blankets, and snacks.

I set the bags on the foot of the bed once I make it back home and watch as True sits up to go through them.

"I only asked for a couple of things, Atlas. What is all this? Why would you buy so much stuff?"

"I went to Target," I shrugged.

"Ahhh, enough said."

No, it wasn't enough said. She said that like everyone who goes there comes out with more than they went in for. Is that a thing with that store? Well, they won't get me again. I'm never going back. She pulls out all the stuff, and she looks like a little kid on Christmas morning admiring her gifts.

"Will you play with me?" she asks, and my mind goes straight to the damn gutter.

I clear my throat before I answer, "Sure. Which game do you want to play first?"

"This one," she says as she holds up the box.

An hour later I am pushing two little cars around the board, and I say two because I have so many children I need two cars to fit them all in. Meanwhile, she only has herself. I narrowed my eyes at her. I think she's cheating, but she won't let me see the instructions to prove it.

"I won!" she yells, pulling me from my internal thoughts.

"Now wait a damn minute," I yell. "How did you get there from way the hell over here," I demand.

She is sitting crisscrossed applesauce in one of my t-shirts and some boxer briefs in her size, smiling at me, and not for the first time, I admire her beauty. "Let me see those damn instructions."

"Nope," she says and begins packing up the game.

"I demand a rematch, and this time I hold the instructions," I tell her.

"Ok, if you can find them," she says. "Want to play another one?"

"Sure," I say, and she sets up another game, but this time I grab the instructions before she can horde them.

"You cheated!" I yell again.

"How Atlas? You have the instructions," she states calmly.

"Then you peeked at the cards," I accuse.

"You have those over there, too, remember?"

Damn, she's right. "There is no way you solved this murder that fucking fast."

"Maybe I'm just that good."

"Nobody's that good," I grumble as I slam the pieces back in the box of yet another game True has beaten me at. I look over at the clock, and I'm surprised to see that we have played right past lunch, and it's damn near dinner. While True goes to the bathroom, I pull out my phone and order pizza.

* * *

I WAKE up the next day to see True in the middle of the bed, eating cold pizza and watching cartoons. Not the cartoons kids watch now. No, she's watching a cartoon about stone statues that come to life and a NYC cop who befriends them. Before I know it, I'm eating pizza, too, while watching the cartoon like a 1950's housewife watches her "stories."

"There's a movie, you know," I tell True during the commercial break.

"Really? Can it be downloaded?"

"No, it's only on VHS tape."

"VHS tape! Where the hell could we get that? And even if we could find it, who still has a working VCR? Damn, I would have loved to see it," she says. Then turns her attention back to the TV once the show comes back on. While she's absorbed in the cartoon, I have ordered the movie and a VCR. They both should be here in two days, thanks to 2-day shipping.

* * *

I WALK into the bedroom after work and find True in a tank top and leggings lying on the sofa, reading from her e-reader. "OMG, how could he trick her into traveling back in time with him? Ooouuu, I'd be pissed, mate or no mate," she says.

I do not think she's talking to me since she has yet to acknowledge me as I sit on the other end of the sofa. "How was work?" she asked me.

"Hot," I say, "but we are making a lot of good progress. We'll come in ahead of schedule."

"That's good, right?" she says, turning to look at me.

"Yes, that means we can move on to the next phase. We have already sold all the houses in this phase. So the sooner we can start the next phase, the sooner we can sell all those houses too. I have to admit I was a little skeptical at first, but my brother, Josh's vision proved to be right. The people around here were just waiting for someone to use all this land to build nicer houses at reasonable prices. Half of the people that bought one of our houses allowed us to purchase their old house, and the plan is to flip those and sell them too. Ingenious. It's a lot of work, but we've provided safe, affordable, upgraded houses for people who wanted them and jobs for people who needed them. It's a win-win situation."

I look at True and see that she really is getting better. There are some things that are still difficult for her to do, which is how I found myself kneeling before her in the shower this morning, shaving her legs since she can't bend down without it hurting her. She put a towel in between her legs like a cloth diaper to cover herself, but that was not enough to stop me from imagining spreading her legs and having a taste. My hands were shaking like a crackhead trying to light a pipe to get a hit. As soon as her legs were shaved and rinsed off, I got out of there like a bat out of hell. It took forever to get my hand to stop shaking. She is going to be the death of me.

"Can I purchase one of the houses?"

I freeze because hell no, she can't buy one of the houses. She belongs here with me. She belongs to me. But instead of saying that, I open my mouth, and "Of course, you can" comes out. It never occurred to me that True might have her own money. I do not know why, but it just never did. "I'll bring you the catalog tomorrow so you can look through it and see if there's anything that you like."

"Ok, thank you, Atlas," she says so softly I almost missed it.

I might bring her the damn catalog, but I will not let True go. But how realistic is that when I still don't know anything about her or why she was left to die? It's time I finally get some answers.

FOUR WEEKS LATER

True

I am almost completely healed. Everything is good except for my ribs; they're still a little sore. I am getting dressed to go out to get a much-needed haircut. My hair has suffered from me not being able to really do it because of my injuries. Atlas has kept it from completely breaking off with the hair products he uses on it and keeping it in braids and silk bonnets. I asked him who taught him to do a black woman's hair, and that is how I found out about his sister, Savvy. He learned to braid from his dad, who is Maori. Although they usually wear their hair down in ponytails or in man-buns they still learned how to braid. Atlas said he thinks their mother missed not having any daughters but pacified her craving by doing her eight sons' long hair.

I need some regular clothes, not more of these sweats, leggings, tank tops, and t-shirts. I have been pretty much in bed and sleeping most of the time, but thankfully those torture sessions called showers came to an end as soon as I got the use of both my eyes back and some strength from regular meals. I know Atlas has been trying to find out information about me and why I was in that house the night he came to kill Victor, but he wouldn't ask me while I was hurt for fear of upsetting me. But I can tell my grace period is about to come to an end. The other week when he asked me my last name I told him the truth, kind of.

"True?" Atlas says.

"Yeah?" I respond while eating salted caramel core ice cream and watching Worf kick someone's ass.

"What's your last name?"

The spoon freezes on its way to my mouth. "Um, North," I say. "North?! True North?"

"Yes, True North."

"That's really your name? True North?"

I sigh a deep breath, "Yes, that is really my name." And I didn't lie, not really. True North is my name, but I don't go by that. I have always used the last name of the parents that raised me, Silva. If I was to give Atlas that name, he would be able to find out who I am and possibly piece together why he found me in that house almost dead. If he looks for True North, I know he won't be able to find anything.

Once he asked me for my name, I knew other questions would begin to follow. His finding out who I am is a real problem. If he knew, would he continue to let me stay here? Or would he put me out? And if he did put me out, where would I go? Victor would definitely come for me, and this time he wouldn't waste time torturing me; he'd just pull the trigger.

It's obvious Atlas hates Victor as much as I do, but I am not sure if our mutual hate for him will be enough for Atlas to overlook my real identity. But it's not just about me. It's about Atlas. Me being who I am puts him in danger, so for better or for worse, I'm going to have to tell him the truth, the whole truth. I just hope I can when the time comes.

I look in the mirror and don't recognize the woman looking back at me. The treatment, trim, and silk press were so needed, and my hair looks healthy again. I went shopping and grabbed some sundresses, jeans, tanks, underwear, flip-flops, and sneakers. Well, damn near a new wardrobe, but considering I have nothing, it was all needed. I opened a bank account online and had my money transferred from the new account I set up that I was supposed to use to start over once I left Texas. Over the years, I have put every penny I've made away in an account no one knew about. My dad would give me a monthly allowance and that went in there too. Knowing what I know now, I know exactly where that money came from. In the beginning, I didn't want to keep it, but then I said fuck it, I deserve that money and more. When I turned 21, I received a million-dollar insurance policy payment that was waiting for me to become of legal age to claim it.

So yeah, I am not poor and I haven't had to work since my dad provided everything for me. That left me more time to train, so training is what I did and hard. I learned as much as I could from anyone who was willing to teach me. I learned hand-to-hand combat, guns, knives, explosives, and poisons. You name it, I learned it. But thanks to my mom, no amount of training could give me the svelte body I always desired. Five feet, six inches and one hundred seventy-two pounds. Well, I fluctuate between size sixteen and eighteen, and on a good day, I might be able to squeeze in a fourteen, but I generally wear oversized clothes to hide my shape. I might be plus-sized, but I have the shape men desire, just super-sized. Hips, ass, and titties made me a target for all the men that were always around my family, so I learned how to hide it. And even though I hide my body in most cases, I know when and how to use it to my advantage.

This sundress I decided to wear on a whim doesn't hide my shape at all. I am honestly not sure why I decided to wear this dress since I am usually a jeans-and-t-shirt type of chick. The only thing I can think of is Atlas. He makes me feel like a woman without even trying. If I could get my stomach to be flat, I'd be a plus-sized baddy, but being around a bunch of men and being raised like a son instead of a daughter, I learned to bury that girly part of myself. So jeans and t-shirts are my security blanket. Atlas texted me to let me know he was outside waiting on me, and I headed out to meet him.

. . .

Atlas

I literally freeze when I lay my eyes on True. Holy fuck, I have seen this woman naked, but this dress shows off her curves in a way her being naked never could. When I fuck her, I want her in this dress, one leg on my shoulder and the other in the crook of my arm up against a wall... hard in this damn dress. I get out and come around the car to open her door. "True, you look good enough to eat," I say to her, and she drops her head so I cannot see her embarrassment. Well fuck that. I want all of her emotions, and I reach out, lifting her face to me. Before she can say anything, I take her mouth. I crush her lips under mine and plunder her mouth thoroughly right there in the doorway of the car. When I finally let her up for air, it takes both of us a minute to get our bearings before I help her in the car and come back around to get in the driver's seat. "Let's go to dinner," I say to her as I pull away from the curb without waiting for her to respond.

CHAPTER EIGHT

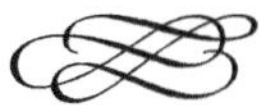

True

   We finally made it back home. *Home?* When did I start thinking of it as home? I go into the room and strip on my way to the bathroom to take a shower. I wrap my hair, secure it with a scarf, put on a shower cap, and step in the shower. That kiss had me dripping wet. My panties were not adequate enough for the reaction Atlas set off inside me. It's been a while since I've been with a man and my body is not happy about it. All of the guys I slept with knew the deal; they were there to scratch an itch, no more, no less. I had zero desire for a relationship, but damn if I don't feel like I am in a full-fledged relationship with Atlas.

He goes to work while I stay home. When he gets home, we have dinner, watch some tv or play some board games, and he still can't beat me. Then we go to bed. He was diligently sleeping on the sofa until one night he was in bed reading to me off the e-reader. My eye was tired of compensating for the loss of an eye, so he offered to read to me. The next thing we knew, we were waking up the next morning wrapped in each other's arms. From that night forward, that is how we slept. We have been dancing around the sexual attraction until today, and I know if we were home when he laid that kiss on me, the aftermath would have been us recovering from multiple orgasms.

Atlas asked me last night if I would come with him to have dinner with his family so I could meet everyone. We are going to the family compound where Atlas really lives, and I am supposed to meet all his brothers and sister-in-law. I'm nervous as hell, but when he asked, he looked like a three-year used to rejection, and I knew I couldn't tell him no.

I turn the water off, wrap myself in a towel, and head into the bedroom to grab the bags I left. I grab the bras and panties set, pop the tag, and slip into them. I put my shea butter body butter on, grab a coral tank top dress, gold sandals, and accessories, and spray on my Baccarat Rouge 540. I pick up the trail of clothes I left in my haste to get to the shower and put them in the laundry basket on my side of the closet. When I walk back into the room, I hear the shower running and realize Atlas is in the shower. I grab my new clothes and begin to put them away in the dresser and closet and realize I thoroughly live with this man. I do not know how long I stand there in the middle of the room in my thoughts until I hear Atlas. He walks up behind me pulls me back to him, splaying his hand on my stomach.

"You look good enough to eat. Like a smorgasbord I can suck, lick, bite and devour until I'm too stuffed to do anything but revel in my satisfaction. Tell me, True, will you let me spread you out on a table and feast on you, baby? Will you let me feed on your love? I bet you taste as sweet and wet as summer berries."

I turn around in his arms and put my arms around his neck, "Don't threaten me with a good time, Atlas, it's been a long time since someone else has given me an orgasm, and I am overdue. You look like you'd give me multiple orgasms. Tell me, Atlas, has a woman ever made you cum more than once? When you cum inside me, will it be so good you stay hard? Or will you be so exhausted one nut will be enough?"

Those green eyes shine with desire and challenge, "I tell you what, fuck dinner, and we can both find out," he says.

Just as I go to open my mouth, his cell phone rings. "Atlas, hurry the fuck up. We're hungry, and Savvy won't let us eat until you get here," the voice says so loud it's like we're both on the phone.

"Fuck off!" Atlas yells back and hangs the phone up, but the mood has been broken. "We'll finish this later," he tells me and heads towards the door.

I am meeting his brothers and sister tonight, and I am nervous as hell. I don't know why I let him talk me into this. Yes, I do. I love him.

I think I fell in love with him the night he rescued me from Victor's house and took care of me even though I was beaten to a pulp and smelled like a sewage plant. I want to be part of his life, and I know his brothers are his life. But what if they don't like me? What if he has to choose between me or them? I know he'll never choose me over his brothers. We decided not to let them know how we really met.

"True,"

"Yeah,"

"My brothers have no idea about my extracurricular activities, and I need it to remain that way."

"Okay," I mean, what else could I say? The man saved my life.

"Let's tell them your car broke down, and I helped you."

With our cover story set, we head toward his real home. When we arrive, my mouth drops open at the sheer enormity of not just the house but the land it's on and all the extras. Who lives like this? He pulls up to his side of the house and cuts the car off. He comes around to help me out and opens the door to his suite of rooms. When I walk in, I am engulfed in his scent, and I relax a little with the familiar scent of him here. We walk towards the main part of the house, and I walk a little behind Atlas, more nervous than ever to meet his other brothers, but Atlas reaches back and pulls me up right next to him.

I can hear the voices from down the hall, and as soon as we reach the living area, my mouth drops open. Well, damn, there is not one ugly brother in the damn bunch. Big and fine is the only thing I can think of. Seven men and one woman all have their eyes on me.

"About damn time," says the owner of the voice that told us to hurry and get there.

"Everyone, this is True. True, these are my dickhead brothers, and that's Savannah or Savvy. She's Joshua's wife."

"Wow, Atlas!" is all I can say. One by one they all come over and introduce themselves to me.

"Let's eat," Joseph says as soon as the introductions are over.

"No, really, what the fuck has been your problem lately?" Joshua asks Joseph.

"I don't know what you're talking about," he says as he fixes his plate.

"The fuck you don't. You've been snapping at people here and at work. And you were just rude as fuck for no reason, so what's the deal?" Joseph sits there and doesn't respond.

"Seph," Savvy says softly. "What's wrong?"

"Nothing!" he yells.

"You're gonna back that shit all the way down or get fucked up at this table. I don't know who the fuck you think you're talking to, but I know it's not my wife. You better check yourself, Joseph, before I have to."

"Whatever," Joseph says, and Joshua goes to reach over the table to snatch his ass up, but Savvy and Atlas stop him. "This is not the time," Savvy tells him.

"The time to get someone back in line is the moment they step the fuck out of line," he says as he stares at Joseph. He finally releases a breath.

"I'm sorry, Savannah. I'm frustrated about another matter, and I am sorry for taking it out on you. Please forgive me."

"Of course, you're forgiven, Seph. You're my brother and I love you."

"Josh, you too, I'm sorry."

"I forgive you, but we are still gonna talk about that shit." He nods his head, and the moment is over.

After a few tense moments, Anson says to me, "Welcome to the real househusbands of Mississippi." Making all of us laugh.

The meal looked amazing; braised beef short ribs over cheesy, creamy polenta, glazed carrots, a salad, and peach lemonade rounded out dinner. We began to fix our plates, and the conversation flowed around the table. I peek over at Joseph, and he seems to be a little better, but he is definitely not as talkative as the others. But it's not my business, and I only mind the business that pays me.

Just as I am about to take another bite, Aryan says, "So, True, are you and my brother an item?"

I look at Atlas but respond, " Um, why?" I ask without answering his question.

"Cause I'd like to take you out to dinner," he says.

"The fuck?" Atlas yells. "Your raggedy-ass isn't going to be taking her anywhere."

"Why not? She didn't say y'all was an item,, and you didn't dispute her. So, she's single and available," he says.

"Well, hell, since we are shooting our shot I wanna take you to a picnic and a movie," Asher says.

"Let me tell you, little shits, something. None of you are taking her any damn where. True is mine." Atlas declares.

"Not until she says she's yours, Atlas. Until then, she is fair game," Joseph chimes in.

"First of all, what the hell am I, a heifer on the auction block? I am not a side of meat to be bid over, that shit might be cute for some women, but it ain't to me. Oh, and by the way, I don't run through families, so thanks for the offer, but I'm gonna have to decline." After a few silent seconds, the silence is broken.

"Well, I think she passes the vibe test," Anson says, and Atlas and I both are looking at his brothers like they're crazy.

"So this was some sort of test?"

"Kinda. We gotta make sure you can stand your ground, can stand up to Atlas, and you are badass enough to be a part of the family."

I frown as I look over to Savvy, whose husband won't even let her pour her own drink and wonder how she got past the vibe test.

"Don't let the smooth taste fool you," Jabarri says. "Savvy is far from a pampered princess."

"Shut up, Jabarri. I'm a pampered Queen. Get it right. I'm just a pampered Queen who can and will whoop ass or put a bullet in a bitch."

I nod my head, but I still have my reservations about Savannah being a badass. Luckily for me, there were no more date requests, but I noticed that Atlas wasn't talking as much as he was before, even though the conversation picked right back up.

Atlas' brothers are amazing and funny, and you can feel the love from the other side of the planet that these brothers have for each other. I don't know why I was so nervous to meet them. They made me feel so welcome and a part of their family. When Jaasiel brought out the caramel apple upside-down cake, I thought I had died and gone to culinary heaven. The cake was amazing, still warm from the oven and gooey with homemade French vanilla ice cream. Before I knew it, I ate three pieces. And this is why my ass can't lose this stomach. I started to push away the plate with the rest of the slice on it, and Atlas pushed it right back to me.

"Eat the cake, True. I like every inch on you exactly where it's at," he whispers in my ear as a shiver makes its way up my spine.

I do eat the rest of the slice, and now I am not fit to do anything but sleep. I lay my head on Atlas's shoulder and pull my feet up and enjoy being here with Atlas and his brothers. He puts his arm around me and repositions my head to his chest as he continues to talk to his brothers. After the fourth yawn I try to hide, Atlas tells his brothers we are going to bed, and Jaasiel tells him he's making breakfast.

"We'll be there," I say before he gets the sentence out.

"It looks like you have another fan," Atlas says as he ushers me to his rooms.

"Good night," I say over my shoulder.

"Good night," they all reply.

Once we make it back to the room, we're both too tired to make good on any of the promises we spoke about earlier, so we both get undressed, get in bed, and go to sleep. There's no rush...I hope.

CHAPTER NINE

$\mathcal{A}$*tlas*

I LIE IN BED, unable to sleep, as the conversation from dinner keeps playing in my mind. Logically I realize that True and I haven't made any promises to each other, but I would think that after all we shared, she would have claimed me. Instead, she was only upset about being treated like a heifer at an auction. Her words, not mine. I know she feels the chemistry we share, the sexual attraction between us. Is she just biding her time until she can leave and resume her life? Does she have someone to go back to? I turn over, again truly bothered by this, and True is sleeping peacefully beside me, obviously not bothered at all. I throw the covers back gently so I won't wake her, throw on some shorts and my slides, and head back down to the kitchen to have another slice of cake and some coffee. Once I have my coffee and cake, I sit at the booth where I was just sitting for dinner, so deep in thought, I don't even turn on any lights.

"I like her," I hear a voice say in the darkness.

"Me too," I say.

"Then, why are you down here in the dark instead of upstairs with her?" Josh asks.

I start to reply, but I don't know what to say.

"You're still feeling some way about her not saying y'all are actually a couple," he says. It was not a question but a statement. I look over to Josh as he sits at the booth with his own cup of coffee and cake, not even surprised he knew what was bothering me.

"I have never brought a woman home, Josh. Never even thought about bringing any woman here around my family, and she didn't claim me, claim *us*," I grumble.

"Atlas, does she know all that?"

"Why does that matter?"

"Don't be stupid, Gummy. You know it matters."

I smile at his use of my childhood nickname. It took me so long to get teeth that when I was a baby, my parents took me to the doctor to see if there was a problem with me. Even when I did finally get a tooth, I only had one for months, and that is how they all came in one tooth at a time—months and months between a new tooth emerging.

Needless to say, I was called Gummy for years. "Josh," I begin.

"Nope, don't try to bullshit me. I knew who Savvy was to me when she ran into me at the airport, and I pursued her until I got her. Not once did she ever have to question her importance in my life, and I did not leave it up to her to try to interpret my actions. I let her know and I showed her. If True is who you really want, and it's obvious that you love her, then man the fuck up and tell her, stop being a bitch sitting in the dark pouting."

I scowl over at him, "Doesn't Savvy need you?"

"Nope, I put Savvy's ass to sleep like I should and came out here to make sure my brother was okay."

Our parents, being close as children, grew up close as adults and made sure to instill the importance and power of what a real family was into us. They taught us that blood doesn't hold us together, love does, and you can love anyone. If that love is pure and you choose to trust your life to them, they are your family. With love, trust, respect, faith, commitment, and hard work, you make your family. It was corny to us as kids, but as adults, I will forever be grateful that not only did our parents instill this in us, they lived it for us all to see. My brother, who saved my life literally and figuratively on so many occasions, is still looking out for me. I really am getting soft as I feel the tears burning in the back of my throat.

"Josh," I say.

"No need for words, brother. What's understood doesn't need to be explained."

I just nod, and he and I quietly eat our cake and drink our coffee, clean up the kitchen, and head back to our respectful areas of the house, never saying another word.

I make my way back to the room and get back in bed, but I am still not able to fall asleep. Even after the conversation I had with Josh, there is so much that still is not clear. Did she not claim for the reasons Josh said, or is it something in her real life she is waiting to go back to? So many possibilities run through my head, and I'm afraid that whatever the answer is to who True really is will be too much for me to accept.

I release another deep breath, and True asks, "What's wrong, Atlas? You've been thinking so loudly it has kept me up."

Wait, so she was never asleep? I'm slipping. I have to start training again and solve this mystery of who she is.

"Why didn't you say we were a couple tonight at dinner when my brother asked you?"

"Really?"

"Yes, True, really."

"Atlas, have you told me we are an item? Am I just supposed to read your mind?"

So Joshua was right. She is unaware of the significance of my actions toward her, and that's my fault.

"No, you are supposed to read my actions," I tell her. "You've been with me for weeks. Hell, I watch cartoons with you and let you win board games."

"Okay, first of all, you don't *let* me win anything. You're just bothered by the fact that you can't beat me. And second of all, how do

I know you don't watch cartoons with all the women you bring back here?"

"Well, for one, I haven't watched a cartoon since I was ten years old, and secondly, I have never brought a woman to this house, let alone to my rooms or bed, only you, True."

"Atlas, what woman wants to embarrass themselves? I didn't know that until just now. You haven't told me anything about your personal life. If you wanted me to claim you, don't you think I should know something about you?"

"I'm so glad you asked, and the answer is no. I claimed you, and the only thing I can one hundred percent be sure of is your first name is True. When are you gonna tell me the whole truth? You're in my house with my family, and I don't know what danger you being here could potentially cause. But I know how I feel about you, and those feelings are growing. I want to know who you are so I can protect my family–so they can get a chance to get someplace safe. Because about you, I cannot describe the level of fucked up I would unleash to protect you, to keep you. I've given you time, True, time to trust me, but I'm putting you on notice. Your time is about up."

She goes to open her mouth, but I stop her, "Don't True. Just think about what I said and come to me with the whole story soon. Please don't let me hear the truth from someone else." I turn over on my stomach and finally go to sleep.

Asher, Uncle Hemi's house is up the street. I tell my little brother to take Aryan and Anson to them. "Where are you going to go, Atlas?" he asks me. "I'm going back to the house to help Dad."

"No, you can't. He told us to go to Uncle Hemi. You can't leave us."

"And you can get them there from here, Dad needs help. I need to go back and help him. You go get Uncle Hemi and get our brothers there safely." I stand and watch my brothers run as fast as they can toward my uncle's house as I turn back. I run all the way there, then I sneak in the door and.....

I jerk awake. It takes a second for me to orient myself. I feel a weight on my back and realize it's True. She has fallen asleep lying across my back. I lie there for a second and get my heartbeat back under control and try to slide out from beneath her gently so I don't wake her. I head straight to use the bathroom. Once I am done, I wash my hands and take care of my other morning needs, then head down to the track to get in a few laps before it's time to eat. By the time I realized it, I had been running around this track for an hour.

I was listening to Busta Rhymes rapping about partying with him. I have no idea how many miles I have run, but I know I am drenched in sweat. I walked for another lap to cool down and then went upstairs to take a shower. By the time I make it downstairs, True is already at the island, stuffing her face and talking to Savvy and my brothers. She looks up at me as I walk into the kitchen. I go straight to the refrigerator and grab some orange juice. When I turn back around, True is up making another plate even though her plate still has food on it. A second later, I realize she is fixing my plate. I stand there, not quite sure what to do, when she looks at me and tells me to sit down. I have never had a woman that wasn't my mother or Savvy fix me a plate. After I take the seat next to where she was sitting, she sets my plate down in front of me, and returns to eating her food.

A few seconds later, Josh walks in, "One of you will have to stay in the office today instead of going on-site," he says.

"Why? What's going on?" Aryan wants to know.

"Jasmine had to call in. She's sick, and it's too late to call for a temp for the day, so one of us will have to stay in the office to answer phones and greet any customers that may wander in." Joshua tells us.

"Josh, we all have teams we are supervising today, and there is no one to fill in for us either."

"Damn, and Savvy has a book signing event she has to go to today, so maybe we'll just close the office today and the clients...."

But Josh never finishes his statement before True speaks up to say, "I can cover for y'all." All eyes fall on her.

"You don't have to do that, True," Joshua says.

"I know I don't, and I know you don't have to trust me, but I would like to help you guys, and it's just for the day. If I run into anything I can't handle, I will either just take a message or call Atlas."

"That's very generous of you, True," Savvy tells her.

"It's really no problem," True says. Joshua looks at me over True's head, giving me a silent warning. Once we're alone, Joshua asks me, "Are you sure about this? We just met her last night, and today she's going to be in the office by herself?"

"True, but you wouldn't know a temp either if you called one in, and you'd trust them," I point out.

"A temp who would have been background checked and drug tested. Besides, do you really know anything about her?"

I don't say anything because, no, I don't know anything about

True. "We can rotate coming into the office to keep an eye on her, Josh. Besides, I don't think she'd do anything wrong to us."

"Are you willing to bet our lives and company on that?" he asks.

I cannot answer. I just look at him.

"That's what I thought," he says and starts to walk away. He turns on his heels and says, "Oh, and by the way, no one is buying that bull-shit story of how the two of you met." With that, he turns back around and walks out of the room.

CHAPTER TEN

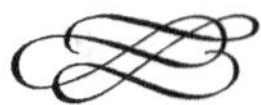

True

I don't know what possessed me to offer to work in their offices today, but the words were out of my mouth before I realized they had even formed. I know Joshua doesn't trust me, and the other brothers probably don't either. But I would never intentionally do anything to hurt any of them. I know I hurt Atlas last night when I didn't claim him in front of his family. But I just froze because I knew once I told him the truth about who I was, he wasn't going to want to have anything to do with me. So I am being selfish and withholding the truth he needs to know. I look over at Atlas as we get ready to leave to go to the other house so I can change clothes and go to the office.

Atlas shows me around the office and gave me a quick review of the computer system Jabarri designed for the office that keeps track of everything from appointments to house schedules and deliveries. He shows me how to operate the phone and how to transfer any pressing emergencies to each brother's phone. Before I know it, I'm alone. The day goes by faster than I thought it would, and suddenly the day is over.

I end up filling in the rest of the week and Atlas and I avoid the relationship conversation like the plague. I enjoy working in the office. It's my first real job, and it makes me consider getting a job or a degree once this whole situation is over. I have money, but I want to discover what I am good at, what I am passionate about, besides guns, knives, bombs, fighting, and killing. I learned those things out of necessity.

As I think about this, I open a browser and begin researching community colleges. I didn't do great in high school; I graduated by the skin of my teeth. Not because I am dumb, only because no one really cared if I went to school or not. When I graduated, no one came to the graduation ceremony. I'm not sure they even knew about it. I'm so deep in concentration I don't notice someone had walked into the office. I have just about chewed my thumbnail off as I look at all the different programs the community college provides. It's overwhelming. I jump and almost fall ass over teakettle when the stranger clears his throat.

I finally get my racing heart under control and look into a pair of crystal-clear, blue eyes. They are so clear they are almost colorless. It's disconcerting. His suit is obviously custom designed, and there is not a hair out of place. His chiseled features all come together to form a stunningly beautiful man. He puts me in the mind of an elf off L.O.T.R., and every hair on my body is standing at attention. I feel like someone dropped a barrel of ants all over me. My palm begins to itch for a gun as I stand and take an involuntary step back. I look around quickly to assess my routes of escape and calculate my only chance is out of the back door.

"I'm sorry to startle you," he says with a snake oil-smile on his perfect face. "I'm interested in possibly building a new home, and I have heard Gideon Brothers are the best in this entire state.

I take a deep breath and retake my seat, I have been around killers my whole life, and this guy is definitely a killer, and he's damn sure not here for a fucking house. The question is, is he here because of me? Or because of the brothers? I have a couple of concealed weapons on me, but that will require me to get closer to him than I'd like, so I take stock of the items on my desk. I have a letter opener, scissors, various pens, pencils, a stapler, and a laptop. If push comes to shove, I'll whoop his ass like I'm a Staples worker and run for my life.

He gives me another creepy ass smile that sends my hackles all the way up and moves closer to me. His dead eyes look me over, and I have to clench my jaw to refrain from honest to god gagging. I pick up the letter opener and begin flipping it through my fingers as he begins to ask me questions.

"Is it possible to meet with the eight brothers? Are they available?"

The fuck? Who asks some shit like that? Even though you can find out on the internet that there are eight brothers who own the company, most people do not know. I reach up to feel the twin hairpin blades I have in my hair. Today will be the last day I do not have a gun on me.

"Unfortunately, no. Normally, their schedule doesn't allow for them to meet all together," I tell him.

"What about Atlas? Is he available?"

Oh, hell no! This shit is too close for comfort. I manage to school my features to give nothing away. "I'm sorry, the owners are on-site today, but I can make an appointment for you if you'd like."

"No, that won't be necessary," he says." I'll stop back in later this week.

"I will tell them you stopped by and to be expecting you sometime this week, Mr.....?"

"Talen Wolf," he says.

Bullshit. "Okay, Mr. Wolf. I'll definitely let them know.

"Thank you...?" he prompts.

"Veronica," I say without thought.

He repeats the name as if he's trying out the taste and weight of it on his tongue. Then, he smirks to let me know he's aware that isn't my name any more than Talen Wolf is his.

I give him a saccharine sweet smile and hold his gaze dead on until he turns and walks out of the office. I do not bother to go to the door to see what he's driving since there are surveillance cameras all over the property and in the surrounding area. I have to tell Atlas what happened today.

I cannot let that man come back in here with the brothers in the dark. Telling Atlas what took place is also going to force my hand in telling him who I am and why he found me in Victor's house, but I was only fooling myself into thinking I was going to be able to continue avoiding it. Thank goodness it's Friday. At least Jasmine will be back on Monday, so they won't be in a bind when Atlas puts my ass out after learning the truth. *How the hell did they find out about Atlas and the company to begin with?*

Atlas and I have been going out more and even took a quick one-day trip to Texas to deal with some of the organizations he is involved with. I was surprised when we walked into a Domestic Violence shelter and learned that Atlas was the biggest financial supporter. I was nervous about going back to Texas even though we didn't even go to my hometown, but apparently, I shouldn't have gone back to Texas, period.

Just as the day is about over, I get a call from Atlas telling me to close down early. There was an accident at the site, and one of the workers had to be rushed to the hospital. I shut down the computers, but not before I save today's footage to the external hard drive and send a digital copy to my email address. After inputting the security code in the computer that will arm the alarm in 90 seconds, I grab my bag and the keys to Atlas's car that he's letting me use and walk out the door. I double-check that the door is locked, hit the unlock on the fob, and get in the car, feeling like I'm being watched.

Once again, I do not show my apprehensions outwardly appearance that I am aware of someone watching me. Instead, I start the car and head towards the hospital. Just like I expected, there is a car making the same turns I am making. I take a route that Atlas took me one day when he took me to see the subdivision they were working on.

I speed up a little, take a turn and pull over. I hurry up and pop the hood, and wait on the passenger side, crouching low to be unseen. A few seconds later, he pulls up behind my car, probably thinking he got lucky. He gets out of the car and walks up to the front of my car, but he doesn't see me. Turning on his heels, he heads back to his car. As soon as he gets in and starts the car, I come up from behind the car and take a hairpin knife out and stab him in the side of his neck.

He grabs his neck to try to stanch the flow of blood. Grabbing the door handle, he tries to get out, but before he can move again, I stab him two more times.

"How did you find me?" I ask.

"I wasn't sure it was you. Someone said they thought they saw you, but he wasn't sure," he gurgles out. "So, we waited in town to see if we would spot you again."

"Did you tell anyone?

"No, I wanted to confirm it was you. Victor would kill me if I was wrong," he says slowly, his words slurring as he loses more blood than he can afford. He barely has any fight left in him, and I carefully reach into the car and grab his phone. I put his thumbprint on the screen to open it. I search his phone, take pictures of his screens with my phone. Using his shirt, I wipe my prints off and toss it back on the passenger seat. I go back to my car, put the hood down, and move it from in front of his car. By the time I get to Talen's car, he's just about dead. I reach in and put his foot on the gas, and use his hand to put the car in gear. I push down, and the car takes off and runs into a tree. I go back to my car and head to the hospital.

Once at the hospital, I learned that one of the guys suffered a broken arm, and a few other ones sustained injuries as the materials came loose and fell on the guys working on that section of the house.

Atlas and the other brothers are pissed. This is a new supplier, and the supplies they sent to be used were a cheaper version than the materials they were shown when the brothers decided to use them. I'm glad I am not the owner of that company because they are out for blood. If the owner has a company after this, I'd be shocked. They have already contacted their lawyer and sent the records of the contract to her. The brothers make sure to keep impeccable records, so I do not know how this guy thinks he is going to weasel out of this.

They also make sure their team is okay and have taken the responsibility of paying all hospital bills and any other bills that may arise for their workers. They have arranged after-hospital care for the ones that need it and will continue to provide pay for as long as they are out due to their injuries. No wonder they keep employees until they retire. Even though I have never had a real job, the reaction of the hospital staff and the workers' families let me know this is not the norm for a company.

It's late by the time we make it back to the compound. After the first day I filled in at the office, it was clear I would be filling in for the rest of the week. Atlas took me by the house to grab some clothes and essentials to stay at the compound, but I missed our house. We grabbed dinner on the way, and everyone went to their perspective sections of the house to wash, unwind and eat. Atlas and I have just finished eating when there is a knock at the door.

"Come in!" Atlas bellows. The door opens, and Savvy saunters in and scrunches up her face.

"What crawled in your ass and died, McPissy?"

"I'm sorry. It's been a long ass day. What's up, sis?"

"Actually, I wanted to know if True felt like going shopping with me tomorrow for a few things for my readers for the book fair I am attending next week?" Atlas groans.

"Shut up, it's not like I'm spending your money unless you are offering."

"Nope," he says before she gets it all the way out of her mouth.

"Then shut up! Well, True, would you like to go with me?"

"Sure, what time?"

"Let's say nine A.M. We can grab breakfast and then go shopping."

"Sounds good."

"Great! Meet me downstairs in the morning. Good night," she says as she heads to her suite.

CHAPTER ELEVEN

Victor

Columbia is as beautiful as I remember. I should come home more often. I sit on the balcony sipping my coffee, wondering what the hell is going on in Texas. My second in command has gotten nowhere with locating True. *Where the hell is she? She has completely disappeared.* I reached out to my guys in Texas to find her and so far, nothing, so I reached out to all my contacts in the surrounding states.

That bitch has to be behind what happened at my compound, and when I find her, I am going to finish what I started. She has to be working with someone. She's not smart enough nor has enough money to be the cause of the small businesses I am losing. It's not that I really care about them. They were no longer serving a purpose, but someone is snatching up the bigger businesses I own. When I found out the casino was seized and sold at auction, I was pissed, and that is when I realized a good fifty percent of my stateside businesses were suddenly gone.

All of this shit happened when I caught that ungrateful bitch at my house, but until I get eyes on her and try to figure out who she is working with, I cannot come to the states. Since my incompetent second can't find one simple woman, I have put up a reward of one million dollars. Someone is bound to come forward with her whereabouts or get me some information on her. Until then, I have to stay where I am and try to protect what's left of my interests which has become even more challenging since my lawyer has come up missing.

If I were a betting man, I'd say he's dead and his body will never be found. Whoever True has hooked up with is good, probably the best I have ever seen, and I am wondering why I haven't run across him before. And I know I haven't because a man as skilled and as deadly as he is would be known in my world and worth more than an entire shipment of product.

I look up over my shoulder as my guards come in to carry the passed-out girl from my bed. I miss the states. the girls were better, it's hard to get the right complexion here. Honor had a beautiful milk chocolate complexion and those eyes of hers were the icing on the cake. When I saw her walking to school, I knew I had to have her, so I did. She is the only woman I have ever loved or ever will love. If only she had listened to me, things would be so much different. I gave her everything she could ask for, and she still betrayed me. I have tried and failed to find her replacement, and only one woman comes close, and she is off limits. The girls in Columbia are too light, too skinny, just too wrong. They aren't my Honor.

The first thing I am going to do when I get back stateside is kill my second-in-command and bury his useless ass right next to Eduardo's dead fat body. I wonder if I can turn this unknown threat and get him to work for me. I could take over the East coast along with the Southeast US with him by my side.

A noise brings me out of my thoughts. "Feed her ass to the sharks," I tell the guards carrying the girl out of my room. "And do it right this time. Last time body parts washed up on shore!" I yell. That incident was inconvenient and costly. I had to pay a hefty sum to the police to look the other way. Here's the bottom line I do not want to accept I will have to go back to Texas whether I have identified the threat or not, or I might not have anything in Texas to go back to.

· · ·

TRUE

I'm ready and downstairs, waiting for Savvy in the morning when I see her come from her suites.

"Hey girl, are you ready to go?" she asks me.

"Yes, ma'am," I tell her as I watch her runway walk towards me in what would be casual on anyone else, but on Savvy, it looks like couture. She stops in front of me and begins to dig in her purse. "Hold on, I forgot.."

"Savvy!" Joshua calls her as he pads out to her with a gun and holster in his hand. "You forgot Brianna." He snatches her up when he's close enough and kisses her breathless, and I damn near swoon. As he begins kissing her neck, she begins to giggle and wiggles out of his arms.

"Stop it, Jag. You're trying to stop me from spending your money."

He smirks at her and says, "You think I give a fuck about you spending my money? Spend it all. We'll live off your money."

"No, the hell we won't!"

"And that is why I am not worried about you spending my money," he laughs. "Besides, I got enough money to take care of you, baby. Buy what you want. I'll see you later," he walks away, but not before he slaps her on her ass.

She places the gun in her purse and heads out of the door.

"Do you always carry a gun with you?" I ask.

"Yep, blame my dad. Since he didn't get any sons, I became his honorary son. He wanted to make sure I knew how to protect myself since I worked jobs that required me to go into people's homes by myself, most of the time in not-so-great neighborhoods. Brianna has saved me on more than one occasion," she tells me.

We get in her SUV and head to town to shop—well, for Savvy to shop, not me. I'm just here to get out of the house.

After a delicious breakfast—but not a Jaasiel breakfast, mind you, we head to the stores, and I see why Joshua wasn't worried about her shopping. She would pick something up, look at the price, and put it back down. In one store, she had an entire shopping cart of stuff. She started to add up her cart and left the whole cart with an associate telling me it was too expensive. I have no idea how she was able to finally buy the stuff she needed for her book event, but she spent that money with no problem. I also noticed she did not have a problem spending money on an outfit for her husband.

We decided to grab a coffee before we headed back to the house. We reach the coffee shop and order our coffee and pastries. As soon as we sat down, Savvy's phone rang.

"Savvy, where are you, Hatima Yangu?"

"Having a nice cup of coffee at Joe Momma Coffee Shop."

"We're on our way," he says, and the phone hangs up.

Less than ten minutes, later all eight of the brothers walk into the coffee shop, and all eyes, men and women, go to the walking wall of pure fineness that just came in. We put together a few more tables and chairs and ended up taking over one side of the coffee shop. Just like at the compound, it turns into a lively event of shit-talking, jokes, and family.

A few of the bold women make their way over to the table to try to shoot their shot. The look on Savvy's face let any woman in a five-mile radius know Josh was completely off-limits. I guess I had a matching look on my face, because all the brothers got hit on except Josh and Atlas.

"I was thinking about barbecuing tonight," Jaasiel says, "if anyone is interested." Everyone said they'd be there, "What about you and True, Atlas?" Jaasiel asks.

"Nope, True, and I have plans tonight," he says, and I shoot my eyes at him since this is the first time I've heard of these plans. He just puts his arm around me and pulls me closer to his side. About an hour later, and god knows how many cups of coffee, frappes, and pastries, we finally leave the coffee shop. With as much money as the brothers spent there, they could close for the day.

Atlas

I have everything set up for my date night with True. I have the screen set up and have hotwired the VCR to play the tape through the projector. I have her snacks on deck: goobers, nachos with jalapeno peppers, and an extra-large blue raspberry Icee. I borrowed Aryan's pickup truck and put an air mattress in the back with some blankets and pillows. Citronella torch candles surround the truck to keep the bugs away, and there's a fire pit lit on either side of the flatbed. The projector is sitting on the top of the truck.

I finish up with everything and go inside to get True. I made her promise to stay inside and not to peek. I blindfold her and lead her outside.

"I swear to goodness, Atlas, if you let me run into something or face plant, I am going to shave your beard off while you sleep!" she threatens as she holds onto me for dear life.

"Like I would let anything happen to you. Stop being so damn dramatic," I tell her. When we get close, I pull the remote out of my back pocket and start the movie. By the time I get her to the truck, the movie is starting. I go behind her and take off the blindfold. Once she gets her bearings, she notices the flatbed set up and turns to look at me with a little awe in her expression and then the theme song for the show begins to play, and she spins around to see the movie version of her new favorite cartoon.

"Oh my gosh, Atlas, how did you do this?" she asks as she scrambles to take off her shoes and climb into the back of the truck.

I take my shoes off and follow her up. Once we got settled, I put her tray table in front of her with her snacks and grabbed my own. I ordered the VHS and VCR and had Jabarri rig the VCR to play through the projector. I point to the projector that's perched over our heads.

"I can't believe you did this." She starts to say more but Goliath's voice cuts her off, and she snaps her attention to the screen, and no other words are spoken. Well, no words are spoken except for words about the movie. She is totally absorbed in the movie and I can't blame her for the cartoon. This is a damn good movie.

As the movie is ending, True says, "I'm in love."

"With who?"

"Goliath, of course," she says, like I should be in a padded room.

"You're in love with a fictional gargoyle?" I look at her like she should have a matching padded room right next to mine.

"Yes," she says with no shame. "He reminds me of you," she says.

"So are you saying you're in love with me, True?" I say, looking into those beautiful, cognac-brown eyes of hers.

"Um, I, I didn't say that," she stutters out.

"Do you love me, M'fhiorghra?"

"What does that mean, Atlas?"

"No, answer my question first," I say, still staring into those amazing eyes. She starts to scoot out of the truck, but I pull her up to me with her straddling me, facing me. I kiss her lips, the tip of her nose, both eyes, and her forehead, and move to her ears where, I ask her the question again. I suck her ear lobe and then nibble her jawline. When I make it back to her mouth, I capture it and make love to it like I want to make love to her. I have one hand in her hair, holding her still as I ravage her mouth. And one hand is on her plump ass, squeezing and grinding her on my cock.

She rips her lips away as she clutches my shoulders. "Oh god, Atlas!" she says as she comes on my cock.

"Fuck this," I say, "tell me to stop True."

"Atlas," she moans out.

"No, baby, I need to hear you say you want this too," I say to her. "Do you want me, baby? Do you want to feel my dick stretching the sugary walls of that hot pussy? Do you need a hard nut, baby?"

"God, yes, Atlas. Yes, please. I want all of that and more. Please, I need you. I want you." Before I can stop her, she rips her shirt off, and the bra follows in record time.

"I'm not a gentle man, True. Can you take me, baby? I don't want to hurt you."

"Atlas, I am not a little woman. I can handle all of you, and if I can't.. I will before it's all said and done."

Before she can blink, I have her out of her jeans and panties. This is not the first time I have seen her naked, but this is different. I know after tonight, I'll never let True leave me, no matter what. I get just as naked as she is, and I watch her eyes when she sees my cock for the first time. I am sure it will be a damn tight fit.

"Don't worry, M'fhiorghra. It will fit. I am not a gentle man to fuck or love, but for you, I'll try to be," I say as I sit up with my back to the back window of the truck. I pull True on my lap, reverse cowgirl style. When she is in my lap with my cock snug between her thighs, I lean in and whisper in her ear. "Tell me one thing, True," I say as I begin to play with and pluck her nipples.

She drops her head back on my shoulder. "What?"

"Do you love me?" I suck on the spot her neck and shoulder meet. She is fighting not to answer the question. True begins to slide her hand to her pussy to rub her clit, but I grab both of her hands and bring them to her breasts.

"Play with these pretty titties, baby. That pussy is mine and off limits to you."

She groans like she's in pain.

"I got you, baby," I say as I begin to make my way to her pussy.

I place both her legs on either side of mine, lift my knees up, and spread my legs. She is wide open and dripping on my balls. I finally reach her steamy pussy and begin rubbing her lips. She is not smooth, there is a fine layer of hair, and I like that shit. I'm not fucking a little girl but a grown-ass woman. I continue rubbing her thighs and pussy lips and even circle her entrance with my finger but I never breach or touch her clit. Her legs are trembling, and her hands fall away from her breasts to cover my hands.

I slap her pussy. "Get your hands back on those titties. I didn't tell you that you could stop playing with them."

"Please, Atlas, I need to come," she begs.

"Tell me what I want to hear, baby," I say. Answer the question. DO. YOU. LOVE. ME?" I run my finger lightly over her clit, and her whole body jumps. "Don't fight it, baby."

"Yes, yes, damn it! I love you, Atlas. I love you so much!"

I place my lips against her ear as I lift her up, line my cock up, "I love you, too." I say as True's pussy swallows my cock. "FUCCK-KK!" I yell as her creamy hot pussy engulfs my cock, and she screams.

We sit here. Neither one of us is moving. The movie went off long ago. All you hear is our breathing and literal crickets. I begin to rub her clit. Placing both of her arms up and behind my head, one of my hands plays with her nipples, the other her clit. True begins to move. Small tight circles at first, then she places both feet on the air mattress and begins riding me.

"Fuck, baby, ride this cock. If it's your cock claim him. Ruin him for anyone else but you."

She rides me harder, and I rub, caressing every inch of her body that I can reach. I pull her head back and kiss the hell out of her, sucking on her tongue and lips. Damn! She tastes delicious. Almost instantly, her riding becomes sloppy, and I know she is close. I wrap one arm around her waist, and the other begins playing with her hot cunt, and she detonates. I am glad we went to the other house because if we were at the compound, everyone would have heard True. I help her slowly come down from her orgasm.

"You didn't cum, " she gasps out.

I lift her off me and lie her down on the mattress, covering her with a blanket.

"I'm far from being done with you."

I jump off the back of the truck and put both fires out. Blowing out the citronella candles, I throw all the food back in the cooler and get in the truck. I drive the truck right up to the door naked as the day I was born, then open the door, throwing the cooler in the house. I snatch True's ass out the back of the truck and head straight to our bedroom.

CHAPTER TWELVE

True

After we made it back to the house, all bets were off. Atlas was like a beast let off his leash. He never lost his erection, so as soon as my back hit the mattress, he was inside me. "You're mine, True.

All of you. I would murder anyone who attempts to get near my pussy." He tells me as he drives into me so hard I'm scooting up the bed. I'm on sensory overload. Him inside me and all around me. He has me caged in with his arms and is laying down so that every possible part of us is touching. It's like our full bodies are making love instead of just our sexual organs. He takes my mouth in a kiss that rolls my orgasm right to the forefront. Tears are leaking out of my eyes that I have screwed shut. The shaking starts in my toes and works its way up my body until even the tips of my hair are shaking.

He releases my mouth. "Damn, baby! She's sucking on this dick. Is she trying to cum, baby?"

"Atlas, please!"

"She doesn't cum until I tell her she can. She hasn't earned it yet."

"Oh god!" I scream.

"You're going to need him," he tells me.

What have I gotten myself into? He pulls out, and you would think my need to cum would die down, but nope, it is still right on the edge. He takes my legs and lifts them straight up. "Cross your ankles," he tells me. When I do, he puts my crossed ankles on his left shoulder and slides back inside me.

"Shit!" My back arches off the bed. He retreats and pounds back inside. I'm moaning, pulling my own hair, and begging for him to let me cum. I've slid all the way to the headboard, and he has one hand on top of the headboard while the other one is on my hip. He begins swiveling his hips against me, and I damn near kick him in the face, but all he does is chuckle. And swivels his hips again. Before I know it, he has a pattern of pumps and swivels that has me promising him anything he wants to let me come.

"I'll give you anything, Atlas. Please let me come. " I sob out. He begins swiveling his hips like he's stirring mother fucking coffee and I know there is nothing that is going to stop this orgasm from happening. He drops his hips, pushing in even deeper and rotates his hips. Before I can comprehend what is happening, the orgasm hits me so hard, it's almost painful, and I literally see stars.

"You've ruined the sheets, baby. We're both soaked. Are you tired, True?" he asks.

I lay there like a cooked noodle. I can barely breathe, let alone respond.

"What's the matter, True? Cat got your tongue?" He takes my legs off his shoulder, pulls out, and sucks a nipple in his mouth. When he's done teasing that nipple, he switches to the other one. *This man still hasn't cum yet. who has this type of stamina? This can't be normal.* He finally leaves my breasts alone. He licks down the side of my torso, and I'm squirm like a worm after a rainstorm. He reaches my hips and licks from the side of my hip to the top of my mound. My pussy is on sensory overload, and just his breath is causing mini- orgasms. Atlas kisses my pussy. A sweet soft kiss right at the top, and it is the sweetest and most erotic thing I have ever experienced. Before I can really blink an eye, he is sucking on my clit like it is the only thing that matters in his world. I try to slam my legs closed, but they hit his broad shoulders instead. My head is shaking from side to side as he takes his time thoroughly eating my pussy. He turns me on my side, never missing a beat. The orgasm is barreling down like a runaway train, and just as it is about to hit, he stops. He lifts my top leg on his arm, then straddles my other leg and slides home. The breath whooshes out of me, and all I can manage is a whimper. I thought I had good sex before, but this...I am ruined. No one else will ever do.

At this angle, he is hitting something on every stroke that I didn't even know was in my body. I swear it is causing me to have one continuous orgasm. My pussy clamps down on his cock, and just like he did me earlier, I snatch his orgasm before he is ready.

"Fuck, True! You feel so fucking good," he exclaims. "Yes, baby, take this nut! Every drop. Oh my fucking goodness. This pussy is phenomenal, and it's mine," he murmurs. Atlas finally pulls out and collapses onto his back. He pulls me to his chest. Straddling him, he slides back inside me. He pulls the duvet over us, and we both fall asleep. I am more terrified than ever to tell him who I truly am. If I was to lose Atlas, I don't know how much of me would make it. I know one thing for sure, I would never be the same.

Atlas

I wake up still inside of True and hard as a brick. Rolling her beneath me, I wake her up with some gentle lovemaking. Her orgasm isn't the earth-stopping ones I was giving up last night. "Good morning," I tell her when we both come down from our mutual orgasms.

"Morning," she replies.

"Hungry?" I ask her.

She rolls her eyes at me. "You know good, and hell well I'm hungry after last night's marathon sex session," she says.

I chuckle and slowly, torturously pull out of her magnificent body, and the evidence of our lovemaking begins to trickle out. Damn! No condom. Not one time did I use a condom with True. I know who True is to me, and even though I never gave any thought to it, I wouldn't mind having a child with True. But it was selfish and inconsiderate of me to have not protected her so she could make the choice concerning a child and her body.

"True, I never wore a condom with you. I'm so sorry, baby. We can go to the pharmacy and pick up a Plan B pill if you want," I reassure her. "That was so selfish of me. I had a complete physical a few months ago, but I can go get a new one as soon as possible. I know I'm clean, and I haven't been with anyone."

Right before my eyes, I watch True's whole mood shift. She grabs the sheet and pulls it almost to her eyes; she's looking anywhere but at me. "Um.... it's fine, Atlas," she murmurs. She begins to climb out of the bed with the sheet around her like a layer of armor.

"Baby, I really am sorry," I feel like day-old pig shit. "If you end up pregnant, you have to know that I would love and want the baby. You know I can take care of it and you."

"Don't worry about it, Atlas," she says as she tries to walk into the bathroom.

I grab her arm, "Don't run away, True. You know I love you and I know I'm older and we haven't discussed this, but I'd love to have a baby with you. You don't want a baby with me?"

"Atlas don't," she says in a tortured voice. "Please just leave it alone." She tries to step away, but I pull her back closer to me with the arm I am still holding.

"Are you planning on leaving me, True? Is that why you don't want to have my baby?"

"Are you serious right now? You act like there is already a baby," she says. All the hurt in her voice was replaced by steel, "As I said, don't worry about it. Now let me go so I can shower. But if you are worried about me having an STD, I will make an appointment at a clinic and get a check-up," she says with an attitude. She snatches her arm away and damn near runs to the bathroom.

"Almost, but not fast enough," I say as I block the bathroom door.

"What the hell is wrong, True? Why are you sad one minute and mad as hell the next? What did I do, and how can I fix it? Are you scared to have a baby right now because of whatever happened at Victor's house?"

"Atlas get the hell out of my way," she yells in my face.

"Not until you tell me what the fuck is going on," I yell back.

"I'm sterile, okay! I can't have kids! So no need to worry about me getting accidentally pregnant," she says as she shoves past me and strides to the bathroom. I turn to look at her as she's closing the bathroom door, "By the way, I would have loved to have had a baby with you." Then she shuts the door in my face.

* * *

I feel lower than shit. It never occurred to me that True didn't have any children because she couldn't have children. And what a weird way to say it. Not that she's barren or infertile. No, she said sterile. I am still standing there looking at the closed door.

When I hear True crying on the other side, I try the knob, and it is unlocked. As I push against the door, I can feel True leaning against it, sitting on the floor. I gently push her and the door until I can get into the bathroom. She looks up at me with tears dripping off her chin. I pick her up and head into the shower with her in my arms. Once the water is adjusted, I wash her and myself quickly, wrap us both in towels and carry her to the spare bedroom. The bed in the main bedroom is destroyed, and everything needs to be changed.

"Talk to me, True. You said sterile. Did someone make you that way?"

She nods her head, and I have to refrain from balling my hands into fists. Whoever did this to her is gonna come up missing.

"I want you to promise that you won't hate me, but I'd hate for you to have to make a promise that I know you are going to break," she says it so brokenly it damn near sends me into a panic.

"I could never hate you, baby," I say.

"Just don't, Atlas. Don't say that. Let me get this story out while I have the nerve, because after I tell you, I know you are going to ask me to leave."

"True…"

"Victor had me chemically sterilized," she says, speaking over me and I freeze at her words.

"Why would he do that?" I ask, my voice dangerously low.

She takes a deep breath, looks at me, and then drops the bomb. "Because I'm his daughter."

CHAPTER THIRTEEN

*T*rue
    "I need a room," I tell the guy at the front desk of the hotel.

"For how many nights, ma'am?"

"For at least two weeks–maybe longer," I say. "Preferably on a higher floor and away from anyone. As a matter of fact, put me in a suite.

"Our suites start at $400.00 a night," Jason says.

I didn't speak. I just looked at him as his nerves overtook him. Finally, he stutters, "Um, I can put you in the Grand Hotel Junior Suite."

A few minutes later, I am in the hotel room looking out on the gulf until I find myself on the floor in the fetal position crying my eyes out. I knew once I told him the truth, he'd no longer want me. He didn't even give me a chance to explain. Once I told him Victor was my father, he got out of bed, walked to the door, and simply said, "I want you gone before I return," and then walked out.

So here I am in this dumb-ass hotel, crying like my whole universe has come to an end. Last night was the most beautiful night of my life, and no, Atlas is not a gentle lover, but he is a thorough and passionate one. I can remember running my fingers along the scar that runs across his face as he made love to my mind, body, and soul and thinking he was the most beautiful man I have ever seen in my life. It went from sugar to shit in four words. I need to go get a cell phone since I left the one Atlas gave me at his house. Tomorrow, I think. I'll do it tomorrow, and I continue to lay on the floor, crying until day gives way to night, and I fall asleep.

Atlas

The door hits the wall so hard it doesn't bother to bounce back. The handle of the door is lodged in the wall. A few seconds later, Savvy comes running around the corner with Brianna in her hand, "What the fuck, Atlas!" she says when she realizes it was me who caused the noise.

She looks at the door, "What the hell, look at.." she trails off when she looks at my face. "Atlas, what happened? What's the matter?" she's holding my face in her hands before she finishes the question.

"Listen, Savvy, I really don't want to talk about it right now. I just want to go to my room and be left alone."

Her face morphs from fine to pissed off in less than a second.

"Yeah, you do that. Go on up to your room and chill. I have an errand to run. If Jag gets back before I do, tell him I'll be back asap and I'm probably gonna need to be bailed out." She turns and begins to walk away.

"Leave it alone, Savannah, please. I just need to lie down and work some shit out in my head. I do not want to have to worry about you or have to take an ass-whooping from your husband when he realizes you need to be bailed out over my bullshit. So please just don't do anything or go anywhere, okay?"

She looks at me—really looks at me, "Okay, Atlas, you get a quick reprieve. But just know that shit is not going to last. I don't know what True did, but she and I will be having a conversation ... soon."

I drag my ass to my bedroom, and I smell her, so I head to the spare bedroom instead. When she dropped the bomb, and I told her to be gone, I went down to the basement and worked out until I heard a car pull up and leave. She took all her stuff. She begged me to let her explain, but what could she say to change the fact that Victor is her dad? I need a few days to try to get my head wrapped around this new information. I lie down on the bed and fall asleep. I didn't go to work the next couple of days and barely got out of bed.

I keep going back to how I found her almost dead in that bedroom, and I am conflicted about if I should have given her an opportunity to explain. But she is the daughter of the man I hate the most in this world. The man I have been hunting since I was ten years old. Has she been collecting information on me for him? I don't know what to believe, and I am hurt. True is the only woman I have ever loved and the only woman I will ever love. Just as I am getting ready to go back to sleep, I hear a commotion coming down the hallway to my room.

"And?" Savvy says.

"Baby, all I am saying is he obviously doesn't want to talk, give him some time," Josh says.

"He's had time, Josh, and I'm over it. He's going to tell me what that bitch did to him, and then I am going to find her, beat her ass, and put a bullet in her! Nobody fucks with my family, my brothers, and walks away unscathed!"

She gets to my door and doesn't bother knocking. She walks right the hell in. "Okay, Atlas. What the hell is going on?" she says.

"She isn't who I thought she was, Savvy, and I am trying to deal with that," I say brokenly.

"What does that mean, Atlas?"

"I mean, she revealed something to me about herself that I do not think I can get past."

"Did she lie to you?" Savvy asks

"No, it was more a lie of omission," I say.

"Hmm. Regarding this lie of omission, did she explain why she kept this crucial part of herself a secret from you?" she asked me.

"No," I say.

"No?" Savvy repeats.

"I asked her to leave," I answer.

"Wait. So this woman has kept a key part of who she is a secret from you, then she finally admits it to you, and before you get clarification, you tell her to leave? This woman who you are in love with?" she asks as she raises her right eyebrow while looking at me like I'm crazy.

"You don't understand, Savvy," I snap.

"Well, I am trying to understand, Atlas!" she snaps back. "Cause that's what people who love each other do. And shut the hell up cause you both love each other, so please don't insult my intelligence by trying to deny it. I do not know how or why you two met."

"I told you how we met," I say.

"Really, Atlas? Do any of us look that stupid? No one believed that story at all. Now as I was saying, I don't know how y'all met, but I feel like you two were meant to meet. I have never seen you so happy. How could you let that go without letting her explain? Explain that to me."

I just look at her cause I really can't tell her without exposing everything I have been up to, so I remain silent.

"Okay, well, I'll give you some advice you didn't ask for. Go get a damn explanation! Real love is rare, Atlas, and if anyone deserves to be loved, it's you. You are an amazing, generous, caring man who deserves to be loved and loved hard. You flew all the way across the globe and risked your life for a woman you didn't even know and damn near ruined my relationship with Jag."

"Baby, I thought you were past that," Josh says as he pulls her back into his body.

"There might be a little resentment still lingering. But the point is you did that for a woman you didn't know. You deserve an explanation, and you deserve to live, Atlas. I mean, really live. You have never done that. Isn't it about time you started? And who better to take that journey with than the woman who loves you. Life is too short; you know that better than most. You and I have had major losses in our lives, and I am so grateful that I got a chance to live a renewed life, and I think this is your chance, too. Find her, Atlas and listen with an open heart, not just open ears. When death finally comes for you, I want you ready to go because your life has been so full, and you have no regrets. Then you walk with death into the afterlife with a full heart.

And if the explanation she gives you isn't good enough, then I will beat her ass and put a bullet in her. I love you, Gummy. Go find your girl," she says as she and Josh walk out of my room.

TRUE

It's been a month since I checked into this hotel. I have had to extend my stay, but I don't care. I miss Atlas so much, I can barely breathe, but I gotta get myself together and move on somehow. I finally went and purchased a cell phone, but I don't know anyone's phone number, so it's basically useless right now. I also got a laptop, so I have to figure out where to go from here. Victor is still out there, no doubt looking for me, so I have to be strategic about where I go from here. When I got caught at his house that night, I had everything planned out except for getting caught.

I changed my name, ordered a new ID, credit cards, and a new bank account. Getting caught threw a hell of a monkey wrench in the plan. So, I've had to reroute those things here so I can make new moves. I search the internet for places I can move to and start over. I still want to go to college and get some kind of degree or certification. I found a community college that I am interested in and applied to it. I have forged high school transcripts that I will send to them and a high school diploma to match. Even though I graduated from high school, my grades were not the best, and I do not want to be traced by using my actual transcripts. The college is in Georgia, a few states over, and I selected Social Work as my major with a minor in Psychology.

Have I bitten off more than I can chew? I don't know, but there is only one way to find out. I want to help other children like me and seeing Atlas do all that work at the DV shelters and within organizations set up to stop and bring awareness to sex trafficking, I now know that I want to do the same. I found a cute three-bedroom, two-bath house for a good price. I picked up a few things from Atlas and his brothers concerning houses, and I reached out to the realtor. I also looked at cars at a local dealership and began the process of purchasing a car. Once I get everything, I will pack up the few belongings I have and move to Georgia.

CHAPTER FOURTEEN

*A*tlas

I didn't immediately get up and go to get the explanation like Savvy told me. I just couldn't face the possibility of that explanation not being good enough. So, I sulked for another few weeks until Joseph came to see me. He walked into my room with food and a pissy attitude.

"I don't know what the fuck happened, and I don't care. All I care about is you getting your ass together and coming out of this fucking room. No matter what has happened to you in your life, you have never let it get to you this much, you used it as motivation. Your brothers are watching you, so get the fuck up, handle your business, and stop acting like a bitch!" he slams the food down. "And by the way, you smell like a wild goat," he says as he stomps out.

He's right. I started this mission when I was ten years old, and I am not about to let this destroy everything I have accomplished. I ate the first real meal I've had in a month. Then, I drag my funky ass to the shower to wash and get presentable. It took me more than an hour to wash, brush my teeth, shave, and tame my hair into a top knot. I might cut this shit. It has grown out of control. I am a jeans, boots, and t-shirt kind of guy, and that didn't change today.

Now dressed in all black, I am ready to face the world again. I head to the one person whose help I need most of all right now. I head over to Jabarri's wing. He's on the third floor. His suite of rooms makes up the entire right side of the floor. Knocking on his office door, I don't wait for him to respond. I saunter in. "Jabarri!" I yell. His office is huge. It would make Tony Stark jealous.

"Over here," he answers. He's at a huge computer desk building what looks to my untrained eyes a supercomputer.

"I need a favor," I say. "I.."

"She's at the Grand Hotel, in the Grand Hotel Junior Suite, room number 1801," he says without looking up.

Well damn. And that is why he is the best at what he does.

"You better hurry up. She's looking at houses in Georgia," he adds.

I turn on my heels and head back out the door, "Thanks Jabarri." *Houses in Georgia! Not until I get my damn answers.* I grab my keys and head into town to finally talk to True. I park my SUV down the street and walk down to the hotel. When I enter the lobby, I immediately spot Peter.

"Atlas, what brings you by?" he asks in surprise.

"There's a guest here I came to see," I reply, after shaking the proffered hand.

'How is my Savvy doing? I haven't been by the compound in a while, and I miss her."

"She's doing well. The book took off, and she is busy with marketing events," I tell him.

"Yes, I bought five hundred copies," he says with no shame. I put them in the welcome baskets that we place in the suites of all my hotels. I always get feedback from the guests about her book," he brags.

"Nice, that's smart marketing," I said, impressed.

Peter scoffs, "I didn't become a multi-billionaire business owner by chance."

"No offense was meant," I assure him.

"Then none was taken. "What's the room number?"

"1801," I say.

"Aww, very pretty. She hasn't left her room except maybe two or three times," he goes over to the desk and grabs an elevator key, and hands it to me. "Tell Savvy I will be there to see her soon," he says and walks off without giving me a chance to respond.

I take the elevator to True's room, nervous about what her explanation could be. Will it be good enough for me to overlook the fact that Victor is her father? *Well, times up.* I find myself outside True's door and one knock is all that stands in the way of being with the woman I love or walking away from her forever. In for a penny and all that.

I am looking at her before I even register, knocking at the door. She looks beautiful, a literal sight for sore eyes, even though it looks like she has lost weight. Hell, who am I to talk? This past month away from her, I lost weight, too.

Her eyes widened, "Atlas, what are you doing here?" My eyes bore into hers.

"I think it's time we have that talk."

"Come in," she moves aside, and I walk in, taking in the suitcases she has in the living room.

"Going somewhere?" I ask as I nod my head in the direction of the suitcases.

"Is that why you came here, Atlas? To discuss my travel habits?"

"No, I suppose not. I came to get answers," I say harsher than I intended to.

"Who says I wanna talk a month later? I begged you to let me explain, and you told me to leave. And a month later, you walk in here uninvited and expect me to just answer questions like I'm a dog being told to speak? I don't think so," she says as she begins walking back towards the door. Before either of us knows what is happening, I am across the room with True pressed up against the door.

"Do you think you can just dismiss me, True? Like I'll leave like a good little boy? I think I've allowed you to think I'm tamable. Let me assure you, I'm not. I said we're going to talk, and that's what the fuck is going to happen. I will get my answers. How I get them is up to you.

If you want to fuck around and find out, I'll be more than happy to teach you some shit today." I growl down in her face.

"You can't make me talk, Atlas. I think you got me fucked up too! Despite the condition you found me in, I am far from a wilting violet.

I run with killers because I am one. And I'm an advanced learner, so we can both fuck around and find out today," she says, ten toes down, looking at me head-on. If this wasn't such a serious conversation, I would have had a hard dick right now.

"Let me explain this to you in simple terms. My only desire in life, since I was ten years old, has been to kill your father. I will call his ass and let him know it was me who fucked up his house, killed his men, and took his daughter. And we will wait right here for him to come to us. Before either of us takes our last breath, you will tell me what I am here to know. You have no idea the lengths I am willing to go, True, and I really don't think you want to fuck around and find out 'cause I ain't got shit to lose."

She pushes against my chest, and I take a step back, allowing her room to move away from the door and take a seat on the sofa.

"Victor saw my mother walking one day on her way to school. She was around fourteen years old. Her mom had just moved to the area, so my mom really didn't know the area or anyone. Victor was climbing the ranks in the cartel when he saw her. He was twenty-two, and she was fourteen, poor, and naive. He began pursuing her, driving her to school and picking her up, buying her stuff, and taking her out to dinner. She went from a nobody to his main chick getting what she wanted, dressing in designer outfits, etc, etc. He took her virginity and put her on birth control since he was so adamant that he didn't want children, even though my mother wanted children. He told her he could take her back to the one-bedroom her mother was still living in if she was unhappy about the no-kids rule. Left with that choice, she did what many women do. She stayed, thinking she'd eventually change his mind. She didn't. She got sick and was given antibiotics, those antibiotics nullified the birth control, and she ended up pregnant. Knowing how Victor felt, she took some money and ran away to have the baby in secret. Victor was pissed, and he looked for my mother, but he couldn't find her. She had a little girl, and in her naïveté, she thought if Victor met the baby, he'd want her. She named the baby True, a play on her name Honor, and took me to meet my father. He took me and gave me to one of his men and had a doctor give my mother a full hysterectomy to ensure she would never have any more kids. My mother was devastated. Not only did he take her little girl away, but she had no idea where. He also took away any chances of her having any other kids. She tried to make it work with him, but too much damage had been done. By this time, Victor had staged a coup and taken over the cartel, so there was no one to stop him or challenge him.

Eventually, my mom turned to drugs to cope and get through the day. It went from occasionally to the point that she couldn't function without being high. Victor tried to get her clean, but she didn't want to be clean, so she kept using. Ultimately, she tried to kill herself by overdosing, but he saved her. It was like he was obsessed with her. He refused to just let her go, no matter how miserable she was, and he also never cheated on her until she tried to OD. After the suicide attempt, he took all protection from her. She was no longer 'Victor's woman', and she up ended being passed around to anyone who wanted her. One day Victor sent for her, and when she didn't come to him he went to her and found her dead, this time she succeeded in her suicide. She never knew what happened to me." She was crying by this point in the story, and I wanted to kill Victor more than ever.

"The man he gave me to ended up giving me to one of Victor's top guards, Manuel. Manuel was married with his own children, and I was raised with his family. Once I grew up, I realized I was different from Manuel, his wife, and his kids. I mean, I was a black girl in a house of Columbians, but it was forbidden to talk about who I was. I snuck after Manuel one day when he went to talk to Victor. I was about twelve or thirteen, and I overheard the conversation about Victor's dead woman and her mother coming for her daughter. I listened to the whole story and eventually figured out that it was my mother, grandmother, and myself they were talking about. Apparently, my mom's mother came looking for Honor. Really it was just because the money my mom used to send to her stopped coming, and she threatened to call the cops and report her missing. Victor had her killed, and he was telling Manuel to get rid of the body."

After a few swallows, she continued, "Victor had killed my whole family. So, I made up my mind to kill him. I began sneaking around and learning all I could about guns, knife fighting, hand-to-hand, explosives–you name it–I learned about it. In the end, Manuel told me he knew what I was up to and began to train me himself. Before he died, he confessed he knew I had followed him that day and that I had heard everything. He felt I needed to know what he was forbidden to tell, but my overhearing the truth, well that was a different ball game.

The night you found me, I had snuck into Victor's house a few days earlier to kill him, but somehow, I'd miscalculated and got caught. He felt I was ungrateful. After all, he'd let me live. So, he took his time beating and torturing me and was going to leave me in that room until I died, but you found me instead. Yes, Victor is my sperm donor, but that's all he is, and I hate him as much as you do. The day he dies will be one of the happiest days of my life." When she finishes, she is in my lap, and I wipe her tears away as she sits quietly in my arms.

"Why didn't you just tell me? Who wouldn't understand after you told them that story? Especially after I told you I loved you? A month apart wasted due to a lack of communication." I sit there rocking her in my arms until she settles down. "Get your shit. Let's go," I say, standing with her in my arms.

"Where are we going?" she asks.

"Home."

We head to the front desk to settle her bill, and no surprise that the bill has been taken care of. Of course, Peter is nowhere to be found.

"Who is Peter?" True asks confused and suspicious by someone paying her bill.

"Peter is Savvy's bonus dad. Trust me. You'll meet him soon." We grab her bags and head home.

CHAPTER FIFTEEN

True

Now that I have told Atlas the truth, I wonder why I was so nervous to tell him in the first place. He asked no questions. He just listened and did not judge me or ask for proof. He hangs a right, and I realize he's taking me to the compound, not the house. I'm a little nervous about how his family will react to me being there. They had to know Atlas and I had not seen each other this past month and probably had questions.

"Listen, True, my family has no idea about Victor or anything related to him, and I want to keep it that way. So let's keep that between us. Oh, they don't believe our cover story, but I don't care; we stick to that story," he says.

"But why? I am sure if you told them, getting to Victor would be easy. We could finally kill him and move on with our lives," I say.

"I have lost enough to Victor, and I refuse to lose anyone else I love. I will not put any of my brothers in danger over this. This is my burden, my promise to keep," he snaps at me.

"What has he taken from you, Atlas?" I ask softly. He takes his eyes off the road quickly to glance at me, and then he's back to watching the road.

"We've had enough heartbreaking revelations today, but soon you'll understand why I will kill Victor even if I have to do it with my last breath," he says, his voice sounding like broken glass on gravel.

I knew he didn't want the brothers to know how we met, but I never imagined they were unaware of everything Atlas had been up to. They seem so attuned to one another. How could they not know?

Before I could slip down that rabbit hole, we were pulling into the compound. The noise level is damn near stadium-level loud when we walk in. There's chaos in the house and the first thing I notice is Savvy running. She has on a tank top and leggings with fuzzy socks. As soon as she spots us, she stops running and begins to slide across the floor. Her slide would make Tom Cruise jealous. She raises a gun and shoots it at Atlas.

"Son of a bitch!" he yells as she hits him in the middle of his forehead with a Nerf gun dart which is stuck to his forehead. She takes no time to gloat as she literally leaps over the sofa and turns in mid-leap to shoot Asher as soon as he clears the door. She's on her hands and knees, peeking around the sofa before she jumps up and runs out the room.

Atlas turns to me with the dart still stuck to his forehead, and it takes everything for me not to literally laugh out loud at him. "Wait right here," he says and stalks away.

A few minutes after he leaves me standing there watching the madness taking place in this house, Joshua and Joseph come running into the room, shooting at each other but missing. Joshua shoots at Joseph and misses, and Joseph returns fire and catches Joshua in the chest.

"You're out!" Joseph says. "Now it's just me and Savvy. Come out, come out, wherever you are!" he yells.

"You won't catch her. We've been training for this," Josh tells Joseph.

"I am Marine Special Services; she has no chance," he gloats, and before the word is completely out of his mouth, he is hit with a rapid succession of darts in the forehead–*that must be her favorite shot*–in the chest and the legs, all from her sniper's nest on the second floor. Joshua roars with laughter. "You were saying?"

"I was distracted," he says petulantly.

"Yeah, distracted, losing," Savvy says as she comes down from the second floor.

"Round two," Aryan yells and everyone scatters.

Before I can make a decision about what to do, here comes Atlas carrying a portable Gatling gun and a couple of other guns, I am guessing for me. He sets his gun up with the stand. *Where in the hell did he get this from?* I think as I watch him. He hands me a few clips for my guns and begins to load his own clip in this gun. He also hands me a Nerf grenade launcher with grenades.

This whole family is crazy. I think as I strap up and prepare to win the round. Aryan has a bow and arrow. Asher has a rocket launcher that shoots honest to god Nerf nukes. Anson has the blaster with night vision goggles that he puts to use when he shuts the breaker off. Joseph has on a whole tactical vest, two handguns, and a shotgun, Jabarri is strapped with a gun that shoots like six Nerf bullets at the same time, and Jassiel is bringing up the rear with his gun that has an upgraded motor and shoots out disks and bullets. I swear they built these damn guns cause I have never seen anything like them in any store that I have ever been in.

An hour later we, are all exhausted sitting at the buffet eating an amazing meal Jaasiel cooked up and laughing at the video Jabarri took of the Nerf gun battle. In the end, Joshua and Savvy won the most rounds. That chick is stealthy. She said she learned how to be that way by trying to eat snacks and meals without her kids knowing. At one point, this chick repelled from the third-floor balcony shooting everything in sight including Joshua, to take home the win. Yeah, this family is crazy, like I said earlier, and I want to live here with them forever.

Atlas

I wake up to the most delicious feeling I have ever felt and look down to watch my cock disappear over and over in True's mouth. I lay there and let her have her way for as long as I can before I have her on her knees pressed up against the headboard holding on as I drive in her wet heat over and over until we are too exhausted to get up and end up falling asleep again. Finally, we are able to get out of bed, take showers and get ready for the day.

True has a lot to take care of today, like contacting the real estate agent and informing her she will not be buying a house in Georgia. It was a cute house, and I am almost tempted to buy it and use it as a rental property or a safe house for women leaving DV situations, kind of like a stop-over where they can get on their feet without having to worry about rent. I'll send a text to Jabarri to make the purchase for me later after I know True has backed out of the sale.

"Why Georgia?" I ask as we eat breakfast leftovers Jassiel put aside for us.

"I wanted to get away, but not too far, and I wanted to go to school too, and the school in Georgia has the program I think I want to take," she informs me around a piece of Portuguese sausage.

"What program is that?"

"Social work and psychology."

My eyebrows reach my hairline on that revelation.

"I want to help girls like my mom and me and all the girls I saw Victor parade in and out of that house. He has not stopped liking young girls. Bastard!" she says vehemently. "And knowing at least some of the work you do, I think I'd like to do the same."

"They don't have those programs at the college here?" I ask.

"I was trying to leave, Atlas, so I didn't check here," she says quietly.

"Well, start looking here, cause you leaving isn't an option," I swear she blushes. *So damn cute.*

"What do you want to do today?"

"Um, you're going to think I'm crazy," she says bashfully.

"Um, do you remember what we walked into last night?" I tell her.

"I'll never forget," she says, laughing.

"Okay then, what do you want to do?"

"The state fair is here, and I have never been to a fair before."

"Say less, let's go."

Why have I never come to one of these before? I am having the time of my life. We rode some rides and played some games. True gave the stuffed animals I won her to little kids as we walked around and ate funnel cake. *Who came up with funnel cake and fried dough? They deserve a whole medal, the Nobel peace prize, or something.* I have spent a grip at this fair, and I couldn't care less. True talked me into going on the Ferris wheel, and we were like teenagers smooching every chance we could get, until we got kicked off.

"I wish Mississippi had an amusement park. I have never been to one of those, either. I bet they are as fun as today, if not more," she says and stuffs her mouth with the cotton candy I bought for her.

Today made me realize all the stuff I missed out on to focus on my vendetta against Victor. When my brothers were out having fun, I was plotting or trying to hurt myself. Our parents didn't know what to do. My brothers had adjusted, but I was just angry. If white-hot rage was a person, it was me. Our mother called Joshua to see if he could reach me. However, he did more than reach me; he saved my life. I had had enough of this life and wanted out, the scar, the dreams, and the guilt—it was too much for me to handle. Josh walked in and found me hanging. He cut me down, gave me CPR, and got me back breathing. Lucky for me, I had just stepped off that chair, and I sucked with knots, so I didn't snap my neck. He never told anyone.

"I will never patronize you by telling you I know what you are going through cause I don't, but I will tell you that you deserve to live. The sacrifice that was made that night for you and my brothers to live should be honored and not thrown away. Whenever you are ready, I will help you hunt that mother fucker down. We will run him to the ground together. Even if that means walking into the pits of hell and taking that bitch over, I will do that for you. I will do that with you because you are my brother, and I love you, and that's what brothers in this family do for one another. Get your shit together, Gummy, and let's eviscerate the fucking coward that destroyed your life. Don't allow him to take your life, too. Do you understand?"

I nodded yes because I couldn't talk, not just from the pain but from the tears.

"Good, now stop getting into trouble, and drinking, and the drugs. You got shit to do, and you can't do it dead or in jail."

We sat on that floor, and I cried and talked, and I never loved my brother more than in that moment. He kept his word and never told a soul, not even our brothers, and I kept my word and never tried to unalive myself again. But I never really lived. I went from angry and suicidal to angry and homicidal. I was never a kid, and today being with True brought that into the spotlight in a way I never paid attention to before.

As we head out of the fairgrounds, I hear a song in the background by OneRepublic, "I Lived," and I think I will take the song's advice. As I really pay attention to the lyrics, I can hear Savvy telling me that I deserve to really live, and she is right. We're going to go to a real amusement park and do all the other stuff True and I didn't get to do as kids because we were both too focused on killing Victor. He took so much from me, but I willingly gave him my childhood, and now I'm going to take that shit back.

CHAPTER SIXTEEN

True

I haven't had this much fun since, well, since last night, and my face hurts from smiling and laughing so much.\y7 We literally spent the whole day at the fair and ate everything we could get our hands on. I am so full I am waddling to the car. As soon as Atlas begins driving, I am out like a light. He wakes me up when we get back home, and all I have the energy to do is shower and faceplant to sleep. I do not bother with pajamas, and neither does Atlas. Both of us are too tired to do anything but blink before sleep claims us.

The next morning I wake to find myself alone in bed. I get up, take care of my morning routine, get dressed, and look for Atlas. I found him in the gym on the heavy bag. I come up and give him a hug from the back. He doesn't flinch, letting me know he was aware of my presence. He hands me some boxing gloves, and I take up position beside him and begin hitting the other heavy bag. We work out on the bags and move to the treadmills, bikes, row machines, and finally, the ring. At first, Atlas takes it easy on me until I roundhouse kick him in the face splitting his lip. Then all bets were off, and he whoops my ass. I held my own, but I am in no way as skilled as Atlas is. Even though he beats the hell out of me, I know beyond a shadow of a doubt he was still handling me with kid gloves. Does that piss me off? Hell no, I would hate for all that six feet, nine inches, three hundred and thirty-five pounds of killer to be directed at me full force. Once again, I find myself on my back in the ring, breathing hard as hell as Atlas stands over me.

"You're pretty good, True. A little tuning up, and you'll be more deadly than you already are," he says as he kneels down in front of me.

Deadly? Yeah, deadly like a common house fly.

"Come on, baby. I wanna show you something." He holds his hand out to me and helps me up.

We walk to the other side of the subterranean level to the weapons room and indoor firing range. They have damn near every type of gun, knife, explosive, and the like down here. Atlas and I practice knife fighting, ax throwing, and sword fighting, which I am not that great at. But Atlas moves like he was trained by a master Samurai. We use throwing stars, and eventually go to the shooting range. He turns on the sound system, and as *Yella Breezy Is Bacc at it Again* blasts, Atlas and I show off our shooting skills. Before we realize it, half the day is gone, and we are starving.

"You and Savvy are two women I would have at my back anytime," he says as we ascend the stairs.

I smile so big I am sure all of my teeth are on display. That's high praise coming from him. At one time, I doubted Savvy was anything but a pampered princess, but Nerf night changed my mind. That chick has serious skills. But I should have known none of these brothers looked like they would ever be able to tolerate a weak woman. And Joshua is larger than life; intimidating is not a sufficient enough description for the man.

There's no Jaasiel meal when we reach the main level, so we have to fend for ourselves, and it seems like we are intruding in Jassiel's private space, being in his kitchen. However, Atlas doesn't seem to care as he makes us a salad with chicken breast that is in the refrigerator. Once he is done, he takes a couple of containers out of the freezer and sets them in a pot of water to heat it up. I realized after a minute that it was frozen soup. So lunch was a salad with chicken and homemade Zuppa Toscana soup, so damn good. He pours me a glass of wine he selected from the wine refrigerator. I am not much of a wine drinker, but this wine is amazing, sweet, and tangy, so good. "What is this wine, Atlas?" I ask after taking another sip.

"It's ice wine," he says. "I usually have a few cases shipped from Niagara Falls. I'm glad you like it." "It's delicious, " I say.

"What are we doing today?" he asks.

"Um, I've never been bowling," I say.

"Bowling," he says with his face scrunched up like he is trying hard and failing to figure out what bowling is.

"Well, let's get dressed and go bowling."

So that's what we did.

Atlas

How much shit had I missed growing up? Bowling? I know what it is, but I have never been and have not taken the time to even pay attention to the rules of the game. But here I am at a bowling alley.

"I am not putting my feet in a pair of shoes someone else has worn, True, not gonna happen," I tell her.

She looks at me and shakes her head like I'm embarrassing her. I pull my phone out,

"Anson, where are you? Can you do me a favor? Can you go buy me and True some bowling shoes and drop them off to us?"

I give him the name of the alley, and thirty minutes later, the whole crew walks in.

"You should have known this was going to happen when you called one of your brothers," she says like I'm dense.

"Well, all of them aren't here. Where is Asher?" I ask.

"On a date," Aryan answers as he sits, putting on his shoes.

"A date? I say.

"Yep, told us not to wait up for him. Aryan says as he waggles his eyebrows.

"Oh lord," Jabarri says.

"I hope this one doesn't turn out to be a stalker like the last one," Anson says as he pulls out his custom bowling ball.

"Stalker?" True says, looking concerned.

"I wish a bitch would," Savvy says as she breezes past us to take a seat. "I wasn't around then, but I am now. She can fuck around and find out if she wants to, she ain't ready for this smoke," she says.

"So bloodthirsty, Hatima Yangu," Josh says before he kisses the hell out of her.

TRUE

Once everyone has their bowling ball picked out and names loaded in the computerized system, the craziness that is Atlas's family commences. Jaasiel won the first game with a 233, and Atlas came in last with a 57. Atlas goes to the bathroom as we set up for game two.

"Whose idea was this?" Atlas growls with a scowl.

Everyone suddenly becomes busy with anything else and pretends Atlas didn't say anything.

"Oh, so now everyone is suddenly deaf?" he says. "Ain't this shit for little kids? So I need bumper rails now, huh?" he adds.

Everyone is trying their best to not laugh.

"Atlas, we're trying to help you out, I mean you are new to bowling. We're trying to even the playing field," Joseph says while trying not to laugh.

"You can kiss my ass. Even that playing field," he says, and we all burst out laughing.

He turns to me as I am wiping tears from my eyes.

"Et tu, True?" he asks.

"I'm sorry, baby," I say while laughing.

"No you're not!" he accuses and honest to god pouts.

It is the cutest thing I have ever seen in my life. He is adorable. He walks up to grab his ball and rolls it down the lane. I swear his ball bounces off the bumper guards like he is playing pinball and not bowling. Finally, it reaches the pins and only knocks down two. When he turns around to look at us, I am holding my stomach as I try not to laugh. He finally gives in and breaks down in tears laughing, and we all join in.

We play five more games, and Atlas gets better with each game. We order the horrible bowling alley food and just enjoy our time together. Eventually, Savvy and I sit out the next games and watch the guys as they bowl and talk shit.

"They are way too competitive for me," Savvy says as she sips her drink.

"Definitely," I say. "Once they started betting on who would win or who could beat scores, I knew it was time for me to have a seat," I tell her.

She looks at me shaking her head in agreement. "Yeah, but I can't wait to see them act out Snow White, and the Seven Dwarfs.

I am recording that shit and putting it on all my social media platforms." Savvy says.

"You're not going to make them go through with that, are you?" I ask Savvy hoping and praying she says yes.

"Hell yes, I am. I worked my ass off so I could win that bet. I wanna see them in full costume and the lines memorized. Hell, I might sell tickets to that." Her head is lying on the back of the booth as she is trying to catch her breath. "Man, that was an epic idea," she sighs.

"You mean you cheated to win that bet?" I ask her.

"Semantics," she says deadpan as she looks at me, and we both double over in laughter.

I watch Atlas as he is carefree and happy, enjoying his brothers, and it feels like something that he doesn't do very often in public. The scar on his face and his size can be off-putting to some, but I don't see any of that stuff. I only see him. It's been that way from the moment he opened the door to the bedroom Victor left me to die in.

"He looks so happy, and it makes me so glad that he found his someone. But if you hurt him in any way, I will bury your ass in a place no one will be able to find you. I love all my brothers but Atlas and Seph hold a special place in my heart, and I will not let you hurt him. He deserves to be happy more than any of his brothers, and if you do that for him, I will be your greatest ally. But if you can't be what he needs, leave him alone now," Savvy says, all humor is gone from her voice.

"I have no intention of hurting him or leaving him. I love him more than I have ever loved another human being," I tell her without any reservation.

"I hope you fully understand what that truly means," she says. But before I can ask her what she means, the cheer that sounds out grabs both of our attention.

"That's it, baby," Josh tells Savvy. "Let's get ready to go," he says as he pulls her out of her seat into his arms.

"Are you hungry?" Atlas asks.

"Yes, this food was horrible," I tell him.

"Let's order takeout and go home," he says as he holds his hand out to me. I take it, and we grab the stuff and head out to our cars. The other bowlers watch us as we leave, and I can only imagine the sight we make. These brothers are big and fine, and if I wasn't with them, I'd want one for myself.

We decide on dinner, and I place the order. We jump in the SUV and head to grab our order. Once we pull up, they bring the food to us.

Atlas tips the girl, who looks awestruck at him as she hands him the food. *Yeah, sweetie, I don't blame you,* I think. As we drive back, the heavens open up and it begins raining. We're not far from the house, but we do not have umbrellas in the car. *Summer Rain* by Carl Thomas comes on the radio, and Atlas starts humming along to the song. Next thing I know, he is pulling over.

"What are you doing?" I ask him.

He doesn't answer. However, he just puts the car in park and comes to my side of the car. He opens the door and holds his hand out to me. I look at him standing in the rain and put my hand in his. He leans in the car and turns the radio up. He leads me to the front of the car, pulls me close to him, and begins to dance. It only takes a few steps to recognize he is dancing the Bachata. He sings the words in my ear as he expertly dances with me in the rain. His footwork is immaculate as he holds me tight and twirls me, pulling me in and away. Basically, turning the dance into foreplay.

I am as wet as this rain by the time the song ends, and the next one begins to play. His hand is cupping the back of my head, and the other is resting on my ass. He doesn't miss a step, no matter what song comes on. He pushes me out into a twirl and pulls me back in with one of his legs in between mine and drags my core up his leg as he pulls me into him. And I cum just like that.

"Atlas, please," I moan, begging him to relieve this need he stoked inside me. When he looks down at me, I become even needier. "I need you," I tell him shamelessly.

He has me out of my shoes and one pant leg. My underwear didn't make it since he tore them off to get to my needy pussy. It happens so fast that I almost miss it, and I'm experiencing it. With no effort at all, he lifts me with one hand as he holds his cock, lowering me until my pussy has taken every single inch. I drop my head to his chest as I bite my lip to try to stifle my wantonness. He doesn't ask me if I am ready as he begins to lift and lower me on his cock. He feels so amazing inside of me, but I remain quiet. He chuckles, "Oh, you want me to work for it?" he asks. He widens his stance and begins to fuck me in earnest. He gets closer to the hood of the SUV.

" Lean back and grab the nudge bar," he tells me.

Once I'm holding the bar, he begins to thrust. At the angle that my body is positioned in, he hits my g-spot with every thrust. "Oh gawd," I yell out. My grip begins to slip, but Atlas gives me no quarter.

"Hold the bar, True," he says as he swivels his hips and grinds into me. "DO. NOT. FUCKING. LET. GO." He grounds out between his clenched teeth. "Every time I am in this pussy, it feels like decadent velvet. I would ask if this pussy belongs to me, but we both know the answer to that question, don't we?" He teases. Pulling out to the tip, he slams back in, causing my hands to slip off the bar. "Don't quit on me now baby. Get your hands back up there." His stroke game never slips as he grabs me so I don't get hurt. I grab the bar again, and he unwraps my legs from his waist, shifting them to his arms. I am wide open, arms and legs shaking as he takes what belongs to him. No finesse, no softness, just pure ownership. "Wrap your arms around my neck, True."

He walks over to the side of the SUV and places my back against the passenger door. My arms and legs are wrapped around him. He holds the top of the SUV with one hand, and the other snakes its way between my legs to begin rubbing my clit.

"What's gonna get me wetter, baby? The rain or you? he asks. "I can feel her sucking at my cock. Is she ready to cum?"

"God, yes!" I moan.

"Stop playing with me, True. Give me what I worked for. Where's my paycheck? I want all my cream."

Between the pounding thrusts he's meting out and his expert fingers on my clit I can't hold back anymore, and I explode. I cum so hard I can't hold onto him, and he catches me before I can slip an inch. He holds still as I recover from my orgasm, and I can barely pull in a full breath. He gathers me in his arms as he steps back and opens the door sitting me in my seat.

"Atlas, I'm gonna mess up your leather," I say as my bare ass meets the seat.

"Fuck that leather," he says as he straightens his clothes and goes to grab my shoe we left on the road in the rain. He gets back in the car and hands me the ruined shoe.

"Good thing we got more than enough for dinner. You're gonna need the nourishment and energy tonight." He looks over at me, and the look lets me know he is not close to being done with me. I remember at that moment he hadn't come yet. He puts the car in gear, and we head home.

Atlas

I wake up with True starfished on her stomach. I think back to last night in the rain and get hard all over again. She got dressed as I drove us home. We snuck in through my personal door and ran and laughed all the way upstairs to my suite. As soon as the bedroom door closed, we were on each other like we hadn't just made love in the rain a few minutes prior. The rain must have gotten to me because I couldn't get through our shower without me slipping into her tight sheath. I pressed her up against the wall of the shower, placed her foot on the bench, and fucked her as I told her all the filthy shit I planned to do to her. And I did every last one last night, and she was eager each and every time I reached for her. I look over at her again and admire her body, she is not a size two or twelve, and I love it. Every inch, every curve, and every pound, I wouldn't trade a damn thing on her. Since she is laid out in my bed like a breakfast platter, I may as well take advantage. I lick her from her ankle up her calf, the back of her knee to her lusciously thick thigh, to the magnificent swell of her ass. I lick up her spine to her ear as I whisper in her ear to wake up as I slide inside her. She whimpers out my name as I pull her right leg higher to get more access to her warm, tight snatch.

"I want to stay in this bed with you all day. Will you stay in bed with me today, baby?" I ask her as I grind into her pushing her into the bed, causing her clit to rub against the sheets. She snatches the sheets in response to the friction I'm causing her.

"Are you gonna make me work for your words again, baby?"

When she does respond, I just chuckle. I pull up on her waist to force her on her knees.

"Stretch those arms out in front of you and keep them there. Arch your back, baby," I tell her. "More," I say as I push on the small of her back to get the arch I am looking for. I spread her knees wider and look at her stretched out and wide open for me. "You look beautiful, baby. Turn your head to the side," I tell her. Once she turns her head to the side, I walk over to her and kneel on the bed where her head is. I take my cock and present it to her, and without asking, she opens her mouth. When I slide my dick in her mouth I involuntarily close my eyes. "Can you taste yourself on my dick, baby? She nods and begins to lift her head, but I stop her. I hold her head as I fuck her mouth, she moans around my cock and swallows, and I damn near cum. I pull out of her mouth to admire her, stretched out on my bed again before I go behind her and work my way inside her slit. I slide in until my balls are pressed snugly against her pussy lips. I go to work inside her, I pull all the way and slide back in. The feeling of her tight cunt slipping over the head of my cock causes me to do it again and again. It isn't until she begins to beg that I slide all the way in and tap on her cervix. She starts to shrink up to get away from these hard solid strokes I'm delivering.

"Don't move, True, or we'll start all over," I tell her as I continue knocking against all her walls.

"I can't, Atlas."

"Are you a quitter, True? You can't handle me, baby? Aww, the baby needs a soft lover? Gentle? You want me to take it easy on you?" I taunt her. She's shaking her head no, and like I knew she would, she gets back in position. I slide the cover off the bed as I stand and drag True by her ankles to the edge of the bed.

"Back in position, baby." She stretches out like before. "Cross your ankles," I tell her, and I stand with a leg on either side of her legs. I push down on her back until I slide back inside the warmest water ride I have ever been on. With her legs crossed, it opens her up even more, and I take advantage of that. I know I am not going to last long, and I don't want to. I place a foot up on the mattress and fuck her like it is the only thing I ever want to do. She is literally dripping off my balls, and I gather some of her liquid heat and coat my thumb. Slowly I begin to work it in her ass until I am knuckle deep. Seeing her stretched, arched, and my thumb fucking her ass, I know I'm gonna blow. Finding her clit I rub just like I know she likes it until she can't hold her position, and I know we are gonna bust together, and we do. Her pussy drains my balls so hard, and fast that I become lightheaded. Sweat is dripping from my forehead to her back as I stand there, trying to catch my breath. The cum snatcher three thousand pussy she has is gonna be the death of me and any man, or woman for that matter, who dares come near it. Our breathing is all that can be heard in the room as we attempt to catch our breath.

It damn near sounds like a cannon was shot when the knocks on the door startle us.

"What?" I yell.

"Jaasiel made brunch. It's family time, jackass. Hurry up!" Asher hollers through the door.

"Fuck off," I yell back as I hear his retreating footsteps. "I guess lying in bed all day is out of the question," I tell True and finally pull out of her.

We make it to the bathroom on noodle legs. There were no issues with us trying to control ourselves, seeing we were both drained. Running through showering and throwing on some clothes. True pulls her hair in a high bun, and we head down to the chaos that is my family.

Atlas

Everyone is at the booth enjoying the food, talking, and having a good time. No one looks up when True and I enter the room. Before long, True and I have our own plates and have joined in the conversation.

"We are so far ahead in the project, why don't we give the crew next week off as thanks? They've been working their asses off. I think they deserve it," Aryan suggests.

"We can do that," Josh says. "It'll be nice to have some time off, and I know the guys won't mind. We'll tell them Monday morning."

We finished breakfast, and we all seemed to have plans or were making plans. I think this next week off is needed not just for the crew but for us as well. We have decided not to take on any new projects for a little while once this next phase is done.

Maybe we need to take a step back from the business altogether. We have good people who can run the business well. I think with us not having anyone steady in our lives, we enjoyed the work, but as I look around the booth, I can tell that it's changing. Joseph is furiously typing away on his phone and damn near knocks the table over, trying to get out of the door. I look over at Josh, who is watching Joseph intently, and I know he's gonna demand answers from him soon. Asher is out the door almost as fast as Joseph. Turning to True to see what she wants to do today, I am interrupted by a phone call, I check the caller ID, and it's Doone. I kiss True on the temple and tell her I'll be right back. Once I am alone, I answer the call. "What's up, Doone?" I say.

"I have the information you asked for, the list of shareholders, and the bank that the business is financed through. I sent it to your email in an encrypted folder. Also, there has been some movement in

Columbia. I'll let you know if and when that movement becomes international," Doone says and hangs the phone up. I stand there for a second, knowing I am almost at the finish line of this long fucked up game I've been playing. This is the last piece of the puzzle outside of Victor's dead corpse at my feet. I want to make sure that there is nothing for anyone in his organization to take over once Victor is gone. I've stopped the girls from coming in. I saw Doone's bust on the news last week. There were a lot of people that went down with that bust including, some governors and senators, male and female. Pieces of shit. The drug line is functioning like a 1978 Gremlin–the car, not the creature. We shut damn near every one of his drug supply lines down.

I didn't work all my life to find this bitch to leave his empire still standing. He took my legacy from me, and I will take everything he's ever worked for from him.

I call my accountant to give instructions to buy the bank that holds the financing to Victor's last business, the real estate company. All of his shareholders will be bought, out or they can come up missing like Victor's lawyer did. Once they are out of the way, it will solely belong to me. I hear the door open behind me since I came outside to take the call from Doone.

"I need a favor," Josh says, and I spin so fast to see what he needs I almost lose my footing. My brother never asks for anything, not just from me but from any of us.

"What do you need?" I ask him.

"I bought tickets for an event tonight I was going to take Savvy to, but she stated she'd rather spend some time alone together, so I am going to take her to the beach house for the week. You and True take the tickets and go in our place."

"Um, okay, sure," I say before I think to ask what the event is. "Thanks. I'm looking forward to having some alone time with Savvy, just reconnecting and relaxing," he says to me as he hands me the tickets and walks back into the house.

I look down at the tickets in my hand, and they are for a black-tie roller skating event. *Black tie roller skating?* Where does Josh find this stuff? I walk back into the house to find True and Savvy still seated at the kitchen booth, drinking tea and eating some of Jaasiel's caramel apple and cinnamon rolls.

"Baby, Josh gave us tickets to a black-tie roller skating event tonight. I'm sure you don't have anything black tie. Maybe you could borrow a dress from Savvy," I suggest.

"I know good, and hell well, you did not tell her to borrow one of my dresses!" Savvy says, like I told her she should dress up as a clown to go. "She should have her own dress that she picked out and feels comfortable and sexy in, preferably with pockets. Don't worry, Atlas, I'll take her shopping. Come on, True. I have Atlas' black card." She grabs True's hand, and they slide out of the booth and head to the door.

"Savvy, where are you going?" Josh asks as he walks out from their suite of rooms.

"To take True shopping for a dress for the roller skating date tonight," she says. "Don't worry, I have Atlas' black card," she runs over to give him a kiss and pulls True out the door in under thirty seconds.

I reach into my pocket and grab my wallet, and sure enough, my black card is missing.

"Josh, how did your wife get my black card?" I say to him, not really caring but curious.

"How the hell do I know? Did you leave your wallet lying around? She told y'all if you kept doing that, she was going to start taking the card she wanted out of y'all wallet," he says as he sits on the sofa and finds something to watch on TV.

I remember that conversation. She was mortified to find out a delivery person had stolen Aryan's wallet that he left on the foyer table. She spazzed out about us being too comfortable leaving our stuff lying around. There is no telling how long she's had my black card. I think, shaking my head. I know she'd never use it, and if she did, Josh would reimburse me, not that I'd take it.

. . .

TRUE

Savvy takes me to the store where she always goes to buy clothes that make her feel sexy.

"I hate looking for clothes at times being a plus-sized woman. If they aren't misshapen, there is always some hideous design or pattern on them. Do I look like I want to look like a giant walking petunia or daffodil? Just because I'm a plus-sized woman does not make me unworthy to dress cute like skinny women," she says as we walk through the door, and I can see why she brought me here. This is an upscale boutique that caters to only plus-sized women. I am not a fashionista, but this store could change that. I go to a rack of black evening gowns to see if I can choose just one dress.

It turns out I could not pick just one dress, and I don't know where I am going to wear an evening gown, but once I saw it and tried it on, I knew I had to have it. For tonight's event, I got a sequined, pink chocolate, off-the-shoulder pants suit. It would be modest on someone else, but on me, it accentuates every feature I try to hide. The fashion assistant helps me pick out the accessories. By the time I make it to the register to pay for my selections, Savvy has swiped Atlas' black card.

"I could have paid for my own things, Savvy. I didn't expect him to pay for my stuff," I tell her, slightly uncomfortable.

"He can pay for these things for you. He expected to pay for your things, or he would've taken his card from me when I told him I had it. It's okay to let him do something nice for you. It doesn't make you a gold digger," she says as she puts the card away and grabs one of the bags.

"Where can I find skates?" I ask Savvy.

"Atlas is taking care of it. Is there anything else you need?" she asks.

"Yes, makeup and shoes to wear. I can't wear the skates there." I say, realizing I haven't worn makeup since before I was caught at Victor's house.

We head to the department store, where I grab everything, makeup, perfume, brushes, blenders, you name it, and a pair of hand-made gold mesh ankle boots. More than a thousand dollars later, we are walking out of the store when I see their salon does brows and lashes. Savvy and I both head in and get ours done. Once we have that completed, we head back to the compound.

"I'm nervous about tonight. Atlas and I have never been out on a real dinner date. Hell, I have never been on a date in my life," I say.

"Never?' she asks incredulously.

"Well, when I was a teenager, but those don't count. I have never been on an adult date. I was focused on other things, and dating wasn't a priority," I tell her.

"You sound like Atlas. There was so much he sacrificed growing up that he pretty much didn't have any type of childhood. You and he are very alike; maybe that's why you are so good for each other. I'm not sure how you guys really met, and I don't care. I am just glad he found you." she says.

I stay quiet because I don't know what to say. Once we get to the house, Savvy pulls me into her section of the house, and it is literally a house within a house. Her walk-in closet and vanity area are the stuff dreams are made of. I shower and get ready there so Atlas cannot see me. I take my time and apply my makeup and flat iron my hair. I am really good at makeup; it was the one really girly indulgence I allowed myself. I had thought about being a makeup artist when I was younger; I used to imagine being a makeup artist to the stars. If I do go to college, once I graduate and begin working with men and women who are victims of domestic violence, I can do their makeup, perhaps to hide the scars and as a way to bring back the beauty that has been stolen from them through acts of violence. I finish up with my makeup and move onto my hair as these thoughts run through my head. By the time I catch myself, I have finished my face on autopilot cause I don't remember doing any of it. I spray some perfume on and take the pants suit out of the garment bag and slip it on. The accessories finish the look, and I am ready to go roller-skating with Atlas.

Savvy comes back and hands me a bra holster and the gun that goes in it. "Just in case," she says. I take a few seconds to clip it in place, and now I'm all set.

Atlas

I'm in the living room with Josh talking.

"Do you even know how to skate?" he asks me.

"Fine time to ask me now, after you give me the damn tickets and True goes and buys an outfit," I say.

"You could've said you couldn't skate when I gave you the tickets."

"True, but even though I never roller skated, I was pretty good at ice skating. It can't be that different." I think out loud.

"Enjoy yourself tonight. I am so glad to see you finally enjoying life and not being so serious all the damn time. I like her. She's good for you."

"I am glad I found her," I replied smiling.

"And how did you find her again?" he asks, one brow raised.

"I told you," I say without looking at him.

"We don't lie to each other, Atlas....Ever. I don't care how you found her. I'm just glad you did. The only person I have seen you allow in is Savvy, even though she did not give you much of a choice." Josh says, chuckling. "Have you told her you love her?"

"Yes," a while ago.

"Have you told her about your past?"

"No," I say quickly.

"How could you be mad at her for not telling you a major part of her life when you haven't told her about your life? Don't you think, at this point, she has the right to know? If you're going to love her and have her love you, you can't be afraid to tell her who you are. Tell her soon, Gummy, and heal together," he tells me.

We sit there in comfortable silence, although I find myself checking my watch and looking at the door every few seconds. A few seconds later, I hear Josh laughing, and I look over at him, scowling.

"What?!" I snap.

"Oh, nothing. I could remember the night of my engagement party and how someone, who shall remain nameless, laughed at me about how anxious I was to see Savvy. Does any of that ring a bell? And you are over here just about coming out of your skin waiting."

"You're enjoying, this aren't you?" I say with a smile.

"I am, but not in the way you are thinking."

Before I can question him about what he means, by that, the door opens, and Savvy walks out. Josh and I both stand.

"Oouuu, don't you look handsome in your black tux with the pocket handkerchief to match True's dress. Y'all are a stunning couple," Savvy tells me, and she grabs me up in a hug.

I hug her back, and when we separate, the sounds of heels hitting the floor has us all turning to see True walk through the door. My damn, she looks like a pink-coated piece of chocolate, and I intend to lick every inch of her because I know firsthand she tastes as good as she looks.

"True, you look extraordinarily beautiful," I tell her when I reach her. The outfit, the hair, and the makeup have her looking like all my wet dreams come to life.

"And you look like a bigger, sexier, meaner version of 007," she tells me.

"Let's go before I take you upstairs and destroy all the work you put in on your hair and makeup."

"Maybe later," True whispers.

"Definitely later," I whisper back.

I take her hand, grab our roller skates, say goodbye to Josh and Savvy, and head to the venue.

CHAPTER SEVENTEEN

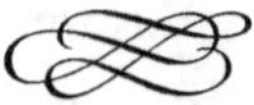

*A*tlas

The venue is amazing. The decor is black and gold. The skating rink is in the middle, and there are tables and booths set up all around the perimeter of the rink. There's a bar, and food is being served while there's a mixture of old-school R&B and today's hip hop playing. True and I are escorted to our reserved booth. We sat and just watch the skaters smoothly gliding around the rink. True looks and smells amazing tonight, and I am looking forward to enjoying this evening with her.

"This looks amazing, Atlas. How did Josh and Savvy find out about this?"

"You'd be surprised by the lengths my brother would go to surprise Savvy and give her unique experiences," I tell her.

Nodding, True says, "Nope, that wouldn't surprise me at all. He loves her to distraction."

"And she loves him back just as much. Let's put our skates on so we can roll out there when we're ready."

When True pulls out her skates, a small gasp leaves her. "How did you do this?" she asks as she holds her pink chocolate and gold custom skates in her hand.

"With Savvy's help. She sent me a picture with the color of your outfit, and I sent it to the custom skate maker. A few hours later, it was delivered to the house."

"Wow," she says. I'm happy to know that I've made a good impression.

Skates on, we nosh on the hors d'oeuvres and sip our drinks that were brought to the table. They must have asked Josh when he made the reservations what his selections were since no one came to take our order.

The first few notes of a song begin to play, and I grab True's hand, pull her out of the booth, and head to the rink. I am a little unsure on my skates at first, but before long, I find my footing, and we glide like silk across the rink. We automatically slide right into place with each other like a lock and key. It's like we have been dancing together for years. She matches me step for step. At one point, she puts her thigh between mine, wraps her arms around me, and lays her head on my chest. I wrap my arms tight around her and send us into a spin. We come out of the spin, and I turn her around so her back is to my chest. I splay my hand on her stomach, and we maneuver around the floor laughing while in total sync with each other.

"I'm hungry," True tells me over the music.

I take her hand, float to the edge of the rink, and lead us to our table. She slips the wheel covers over her wheels so she can walk on the skates.

"I have to use the restroom," she says as she leans over and kisses me before she walks off.

TRUE

This whole night has been amazing, and I am thoroughly enjoying myself. When Atlas first hit the rink floor and wobbled a little, I thought, *finally, there's something he's not good at.* That lasted all of ninety seconds, and then he was like Cab Calloway on skates. When I get to the restroom, there is a small line, so I take my place and wait. It's a good thing I don't have to pee bad. Finally, I got into an empty stall. This is the only thing I hate about these one-piece pants-suits you have to damn strip naked to use the bathroom. Just as I am finishing up, I tune into the voices at the sink.

"Did you see that giant out there?" the voice says, and I smile because I know they are talking about Atlas. He was the biggest man out there, and he definitely stood out.

"Yeah, I saw him," another voice says. "Who could miss that much man? And he was smooth on the floor."

"Yes, but then I caught a look at his face!" a third voice chimes in.

"Girl, someone fucked his face up!"

"Yeah, they did," the first voice says. "I wouldn't be caught dead out in public with Frankenstein."

They all start laughing, and I am so pissed I cannot even think straight.

"I wonder how he got that woman to be seen in public with him? She's not ugly at all."

"But she's fat. He probably has money. The tickets to this event weren't cheap."

"I wouldn't say she's fat, but she is on the thicker side of life," one of the voices says. "When I think of fat, I do not think of her shape. She is the definition of coke bottle shaped."

"Yeah, super-sized," another voice says, and they all laugh.

I walk out of the stall, and they all freeze in horror. It is obvious they didn't know I was in the restroom with them. I walk to the sink and wash my hands calmly and deliberately as I try to get my anger under control.

"Well, since we all know you heard us, why don't you tell us how Frankenstein got you to come out in public with him?" This trick that looks like the business end of a mule says to me, and before I can catch myself I slap the bitch clean off her feet.

"I guess y'all mommas ain't never told you that everyone you play with ain't playing with you. I will calmly slice your neck open, pull your tongues out of the hole and tie that mother fucker in a knot for speaking about that man. And will happily sit in jail for murder over him," I tell the three women as the one I slapped tries to get back up on her feet.

"Bitch ain't nobody scared of you; I'm from New York City. I fought every day," she says.

Well, this night is not going to go like I thought it was going to go I think. "I don't give a fuck where you grew up. Nobody talks about my man and just walks away without repercussions. He is more man than any one of your men put together times infinity. You wish you could have him. And no, he didn't have to pay me to do anything with him. It is always my pleasure to be in his presence, but his big dick is always an extra incentive to be with him. Maybe if your man had a big dick, your ignorant ass would have other things to focus on besides someone else's man. But all of your personalities are giving off small dick, ashy knees energy. It's giving dry fish fry pussy energy for me. Long neck, no ass, gap-tooth bitch."

Atlas

True, it takes a long time in the bathroom, but there is usually a line at the women's restroom, so I give her a few more minutes. After a few more minutes go by, I get up to see if she is okay, and a woman runs into me, as she literally runs from the direction of the restroom. I pick up my pace to the restroom and hear True defend me to whoever she is talking to. The next thing I know, it sounds like a battle is taking place. I don't think twice. I walk right in because if True is in trouble, female or not, I'm fucking someone up. I open the door and stop in my tracks as I watch True dog walking a woman. Two other women are on the floor in various levels of fucked up. The last woman True is fucking up looks like she wants to be done with this fight, and every time she tries to get away, True snatches her ass back.

There are hair tracks, wigs, fabric, and jewelry scattered all over the bathroom. I stand and watch as True reaches back and punches the woman in the face so hard she knocks her ass out. My dick is hard. That shit is sexy as hell. I gotta apologize to Josh. I used to think he was crazy when he gets turned on whenever Savvy does anything badass. True turns to look at me, and she still looks perfect, not one hair out of place, no bruises or scars, and her clothes are not torn or even wrinkled. I look at the three women on the bathroom floor and they look like they've been run over by a bulldozer.

"Baby," I say and hold my arms out to her and she walks right into them.

"They deserved it," she says.

"I have no doubt," I say. "Come on, let's go wait for the cops."

An hour later, we are in the car heading home. The cops and paramedics came because those women definitely needed medical attention and took our statements along with the other women who were in the bathroom with True. The other women confirmed that the three women tried to jump True, and she defended herself. Those women fucked around and found out that True was the wrong one to try to jump. She is a trained killer that was raised in one of the largest and deadliest drug cartels in the US.

"I have something for you when we get home," I tell her.

"I'm sorry I ruined our night together," she says remorsefully.

"First of all, our night is not over, and second of all, you didn't ruin anything," I tell her.

When we get back to the compound, I pull up to the party house we built for Savvy and Josh's wedding. Once we get inside, I turn on the tea lights and the sound system.

"Put your skates back on," I tell her.

Once we both have on our skates, we dance around the dance floor to the neo-soul pouring out of the sound system.

I shrug out of my jacket and toss off the dance floor along with my tie. Pulling True to me, I take her mouth in a blistering kiss. She begins to unbutton my shirt and pulls it out of my pants and off my shoulders. It goes in the same direction as the suit coat, along with the tee shirt I had on. My belt is off next, zipper and button on my pants and when she pushes them down, she frowns as she tries to figure out how to get them over my skates.

I bring her back up to me. "Don't worry about my pants, baby," I tell her as I begin to unzip her pantsuit. When it drops to her waist, I notice the bra holster, and if my cock wasn't already hard, it would have been titanium hard at this point. "Baby, where did you get this from?" I ask as I glide my finger around it.

"Savvy," she says breathlessly. *Figures,* I think.

"How are we supposed to get our clothes the rest of the way off?" she says as she strokes my cock. "Anxious?" I tease her.

"Yes, I am soaking wet, Atlas. I need you," she moans.

"Are you, baby?" I reach between us and slip her panty to the side and rub her fat slick lips. "Hmmm," I say as I lick my fingers tasting her desire on my fingers. I lean down and grab my knife out of my pants pocket. I proceed to cut our clothes the rest of the way off.

"Atlas!"

"I'll buy you another one in every color," I say roughly. I don't bother cutting her panties, I simply snatch them off her body. I gather our ruined clothes and skate over to the tables. I throw our clothes on a table and grab two chairs. I skate to the middle of the dance floor and place one chair in front of the other, facing each other.

"Come here, baby."

True skates over to me.

"Sit down."

Once she does, I take the seat in front of her. She reaches back to take off her bra.

"Leave it on and the holster," I whisper to her. "Open, baby." She opens her legs with no shame.

"Wider."

And she does. Her pretty pussy is open wide, glistening, and wet.

"Pull your bra down. Let me see those beautiful nipples love." She pulls the cups down, and those glorious tits fall free, and I can't help but lean forward and take them in my mouth. I suck, nibble, and lick her nipples until True is damn near dripping on the seat. She grabs my hair, and I release her nipples. "Grab the side of the chair, and keep them there," I snapped at her.

"I want to touch you too, Atlas," she begs me.

"You will, baby, later. Don't worry. You'll be very busy touching me. Now grab the side of the damn chair."

Once she puts her hands where I tell her, I go back to enjoying her breasts. She is squirming on the chair, begging me with her body to do more. Let her do more. I leave her breasts alone and sit back in my chair.

"You're soaked, baby. Do you need to cum?"

"You know I do," she snaps at me.

"Touch yourself, baby. Let me see how you play with that pussy when you think of me."

"Atlas, I can't. I, I…. it's embarrassing!" she stutters out.

I run my finger through her pussy lips and take the juice, and spread it over my cock. I do this a few times until my cock is covered in her juices, and I begin to stroke my cock, and I watch her. "I never want you to be embarrassed with me, love. Now play with my pussy. I want to see her sucking on your finger, wishing it was my cock, I want to see you explode when your body can't take it anymore, but it is not enough because I'm not the one inside you, stroking you, bringing your pleasure. Come on, baby, play with her, make love to my pussy like you want me to."

She touches her pussy and moans immediately, she rubs her clit, and very quickly, she is on the verge of cumming.

"Don't come yet!" I tell her sharply.

"Please," she whines.

"I said no, True. Fuck yourself. Slide a finger inside that honey pussy and fuck yourself, hard."

"Oh my gawd," she cries out at my words as she slides her finger inside her pussy. I sit in front of her, stroking my cock as she finger fucks herself. She is begging and damn near in tears with need. I stop stroking my cock and slide a finger inside her with her finger and help her.

"Does that help, baby?"

"No," she yells.

I remove my finger and put another finger in. She slides down a little in the chair.

"Better?"

"No."

"Put another finger in."

She slides down to the edge of the seat. Her head is back, her mouth open, and tears are sliding down her face.

"You've got three fingers inside you, baby. Does it feel like my cock, baby?"

"No."

"Well, you'll get the real thing soon," I say, chuckling. "I heard you, True," I tell her and she snaps her head up to look at me. Her eyes are glazed over, and she is barely keeping up with the conversation. In the bathroom with those women, I didn't hear what they were saying to you, but I heard what you said to them about me. And then, when I walked in and witnessed you handing them their asses, my dick was harder than it's ever been in my life! Keep stroking, baby, don't stop," I tell her. "I am going to fuck you, True, and it won't be pretty or soft, but it will be with love."

She is looking at me with so much love it's almost overwhelming. I cannot believe I almost willingly excluded this from my life, being so focused on my revenge. At my words, she cums hard. Fuck this, I pull her up from the chair, and she almost falls to her knees. Her legs are so weak from her orgasm. I hold her to me and skate us away from the chairs. I lean down, pick her up, flip her, and dive in her pussy. She has a thigh on each shoulder and she slaps my thighs as I completely devour her pussy, and fuck her with my tongue. "Atlas!' she screams.

"If you had my cock in your mouth, you wouldn't be able to scream True," I tell her when I release my treat.

I go back to sucking on her plump lips, and she swallows my cock and it's my turn to yell out.

We enjoy each other in our skates on the dance floor under the stars. I begin to slowly skate us around the floor, but when True takes my cock down to the root and swallows, I know I am just about to give in and cum down her throat. I suck her clit into my mouth, lightly bite it, and flick it with my tongue at the same time and she explodes. She damn near chokes since my cock was down her throat at the time, but she recovers quickly. I flip her upright and lower her onto my cock, and we both whimper at the feeling. I am still skating us around the dance floor as I fuck True. I kiss her gently as I fuck her hard. She is pulling my hair and begging me for more. How did I find this woman who is my perfect mate in every way? I know it was meant for me to find her. Even though I did not kill Victor that night, I found my mate, my partner, in every way. I skate us to the tables and lay True on top of it, I pull out of her heat long enough to take off the skates and plunge back inside of her. I am going to have to come back in here later and throw all the furniture we fucked up away. *This table ain't gonna make it either*, I think, and I put one of True's legs on my shoulder, grip the edge of the table and fuck her like I have been wanting to all night. I suck her nipples, bite her neck, pull her hair. I flip her ass over like a flapjack as I tell her with my body that she is mine, her body, her mind, her heart, her soul, it all belongs to me, and I am hers willingly. Her skates are missing. She has one leg on the table and the other on the floor. I play with her clit and squeeze her throat, her pussy begins an internal massage, and I know I'm at the end of my rope. I snatch her ass up off the table, walk her over to the wall, lift her up, and drop her on my cock. I lift her and drop her over and over until she locks her ankles behind my back and begins to lift and drop herself using the wall as leverage. I grab her neck and force her to look at me as I squeeze. Her eyes grow big for a second before they glaze over.

"I'm gonna fuck your ass soon, True. I am going to fuck it hard the same way I fuck this pussy, and you are going to take it, and you're going to love it. Do you want my cock forcing its way into your fat ass? You like a little pain with your pleasure, don't you, baby?" And just like I knew it would, her pussy clamps down on me, I squeeze her neck harder, and we detonate together. I switch positions and place my back on the wall and slide us down to the floor. I am still inside her, and we are both completely out of breath.

"I love you, baby." I proclaim, but when she doesn't respond, I start to panic until I realize she's fallen asleep. I notice my suit coat not far away. I grab it, cover True as much as I can, and fall asleep still inside her with her in my arms.

CHAPTER EIGHTEEN

rue

I wake up extra groggy, but Atlas is adamant I wake up.

"What the hell are you talking about?" I grumble.

"Get up, baby. We have something to do," he urges me.

"Atlas, it is oh dark thirty. Why are we getting up?"

"It is four pm, not oh dark thirty. You have slept all day," he laughs.

"And you kept me up all last night, so we're even," I tell him.

"So you don't want to get up and go with me?" He sounds like a three-year-old.

I turn over and look at him, and he looks so damn cute. I know I lost the battle. I just get up and go to get dressed. Thirty minutes later, he is literally dragging me outside to the backyard, and I can only blink at the sight before me.

"Are you serious right now?" I ask him.

He finally stops dragging me and turns to look at me crestfallen.

"You don't want to go with me?" he asks in a small voice.

Jesus, be a fence. When did he start sounding and looking like a little boy? There is no way I can tell him no. "It's not that I do not want to go, Atlas. How the hell did you get that here? Did you buy it?" I ask, one brow lifted as I squint at him.

"No, I didn't buy it. I rented it for us."

"Well let's go."

We walk over to an honest to god hot air balloon in all its rainbow-colored beauty. Atlas gets in first and helps me in, and the operator gets to work getting us in the air. The basket is bigger than I expected, and there are chairs and a small table set up with a picnic basket. Of course, my stomach growls right on cue. We take a seat and take the food out of the picnic basket. As soon as I bite into the food, I know Jaasiel cooked it. We dig in while flying over the Gulf of Mexico, eating, talking, and enjoying each other's company.

Victor

The incompetence that surrounds me is astonishing. I have lost damn near everything that I own in the United States, EVERYTHING! My partners are coming up missing, arrested, or refusing to work with me any longer. And despite the reward I put up for information concerning True's whereabouts, there has been nothing but false leads filtering in. I had my second-in-command fly in today so that I could get answers directly from him. I pace on my balcony as I await his arrival. Little does he know if he doesn't give me satisfactory answers, I will kill him and his whole family. I had them picked up and flown in right after he left to come here. While he's been dragging his feet trying to avoid facing me, his family has been brought here and is locked in one of the bedrooms. Finally, I see him pulling up. He notices me as soon as he steps out of the car with a gun in my hand. "Well, what do you have to tell me?" I bark at him without preamble.

"True has not been seen anywhere, I sent men to the surrounding states, and no one has seen her. However, there is one guy who went to Mississippi and never returned. When I ask questions about the arrests and the seizures, it all leads back to the DEA. The smaller businesses have been donated to DV shelters around the southern states. "

He stands there looking at me like he's told me some valuable information. "So a man went to Mississippi and decided not to come back to tell you he didn't find anything is all you have to report? And where have you personally looked?"

"Me?" he squeaks out. "I was keeping your other businesses running," he tells me as he begins to fidget.

"What business?" I thunder out. "I don't have any more businesses, save the real estate company, and how long do you think that's going to last?!" I scream in his face.

"I will go home and make sure nothing happens to the real estate company," he rushes out as he begins to back out of the room. I let him go to think he's going to get away. As soon as he clears the door, he damn near runs down the stairs. As he is making his escape, I go next door to where his family is bound and gagged. I untie his son and walk him out on the balcony. His father is just getting to the car when I call his name. He spins around and looks up to where we are, and freezes. His son is crying, and on cue, he begins begging for his son's life.

"I gave you months to find True and whoever is dismantling my organization and you come to me with nothing! I cannot let this level of incompetence slide, especially from my second-in-command."

"Please, Victor, he has nothing to do with it. Kill me but let my son live."

I take the tape off of his son's mouth. "Tell me, Alejandro, if I kill your father here today, will you one day avenge him by killing me?" I ask his son. And like I knew he would, he says he would.

"You know how I operate. I never leave anyone behind to come after me. I do not have to look over my shoulder."

"Well, you obviously didn't kill everyone. Someone is coming after you, and from the looks of it, he's going to find you after he finishes taking everything you hold dear. You would have killed your own daughter, you fuck little girls, you're a sick fuck, and I hope he kills you!" he screams up at me.

I point the gun and shoot his son and toss his body off the balcony. He wails in grief, and he cradles his son in his arms. Before he can gather himself to come inside and possibly try to kill me, I grab another family member, his wife. When he looks up again and sees her with me, I know he understands what is about to happen. He will not make it back to the US, and neither will any member of his family. There will be no bodies buried, we'll have a good ole fashioned bonfire tonight, and I intend to roast a whole bag of marshmallows with it. I don't enjoy killing, nor do I dislike it. I have no feeling about it at all. I let him try to run for it, but he stands his ground surrounded by his family's dead bodies. I waste no time playing with him and put a bullet between his eyes. Fuck this. It's time to go home and face this boogyman head-on.

TRUE

I wake with a start and sit quietly to try and figure out what it was that woke me up when I realize it's Atlas. He is having a nightmare, he's talking, but I can't make out what he is saying, but he is crying.

"Atlas," I say while I gently shake him to try to wake him up.

"Atlas, baby wake up."

I recall many nights that I thought I heard him talking in his sleep and just thought I was imagining things. I reach over and wipe his eyes and call his name again, and before I can get his whole name out, he grabs me and holds me to him while he cries gut-wrenching tears. I had no idea what he was dreaming about, but I ended up crying with him and comforting him as best I could. We lay in bed for hours, just holding each other and healing each other with our presence and love.

We finally got out of bed, got dressed, and headed out to eat. As we were driving, I suddenly found myself sliding across the seat as Atlas made a sharp right into a plaza parking lot.

"Where are we going?" I ask him as I squint, looking out of the windshield.

"I heard about this place from some of the guys I work with, I want to try it," he says as he finds a place to park.

"This looks like a children's place, baby. There's a giant mouse on the front. You can't be serious," I say, looking at him like he has grown two heads. He pays no attention to me as he gets out and comes around to help me out of the SUV.

"Atlas?" I say to try to reason with him. All that gets me is dragged inside. When we walk in, with no kids with us, people look at us like we're crazy, which Atlas ignores. He finds us a booth and orders us two large pizzas and fifty dollars in tokens. Two hours later, we've eaten both pizzas, drank three pitchers of pop, and used almost all our tokens. I am doubled over in laughter looking at Atlas on his knees in front of the skeeball games because his big ass is too tall to play the game. At this point, he's throwing the ball and not rolling it.

"Cheater!" I yell.

A little girl comes up to him and tells him, "You know you're supposed to roll the ball and not throw it. You're going to get in trouble and have to sit in timeout for that," and walks away but not before Atlas sticks his tongue out at her.

"Really, Atlas?"

"She started it!"

"Wow," I say as I walk away.

We take our tickets to the prize counter and pick out gifts for ourselves and the family. We grab our bounty and head out to the car.

"Thank you, baby. I was a little worried at first, but I am glad you forced me to try it out."

"I knew it would be fun. If kids always want to go it must be fun to go to. He tells me as we head home. We sit in silence, listening to the music he's streaming from his phone.

"True, what are you going to do after all of this is over?"

"What do you mean?"

"I mean, once Victor is gone, what are our plans? Are you willing to stay here with me? Will you leave to live the life you planned if you had been successful in killing Victor? I want you to stay with me, but obviously, that decision would be up to you," he says.

"Honestly, I was looking into going to colleges here so I could get that degree we talked about, and I wanted to work in DV shelters either with you or start my own," I said bashfully.

"Hmm, I would be more than happy to help you open and operate a DV shelter here in Mississippi and possibly expand into Georgia and Texas. Did you apply to school yet? "No, not yet" I said with excitement bubbling up inside me. "I think you should asap, but you don't have to wait to get your degree to begin working towards opening a shelter. We can buy an existing building, or we can build it for you. Also, I am sure all the brothers would like to be a part of something like this, or it could just be ours. Think about it and let me know what you would like to do, okay?"

"Okay," I say.

He has put so much out there that thoughts are swimming in my head, making it hard to focus on just one. Having the brothers involved would open a lot of doors, not just with financing but with exposure and support.

"Do all the shelters have to have all the brothers involved, or can I start with everyone and expand and have a shelter be just ours?"

"Even if all the brothers are involved, their participation can be as little or as much as you want it to be. They would never overstep. This is your project, your baby," he says. "But I think the Mississippi chapter of True's Shelter would benefit greatly from all the brothers' involvement."

We continue talking about the particulars of the shelter as we head home. Atlas stops in the middle of his sentence and turns the music up. Once the song goes off, he hits replay on his phone.

"Did you listen to this song?"

"Not really," I say.

"I did, and it is everything I feel about you. Listen to the words," he implores.

So I do. By the time the song is over, I am in tears and gazing at him with all the love I feel for him. Is Atlas a nice man? To other people, no, but he is my knight in shining armor. He is everything I didn't know I wanted or needed in my life.

If I had to go through that beating just to meet him, I would do it a million times just to get to him. The scar and the attitude, if other people couldn't see past it, they have severely cheated themselves because Atlas is the type of man anyone would love to have in their corner. And the type of man that any woman would be proud to claim as her own. The words of the song match both of us and say exactly how I feel for him too. God, I love this man. He has shown me another side of life. A side where I am accepted, where family is a real thing, and that I am worthy of a real, bone-deep love.

"What is the name of the song, Atlas?"

"'Next to Me' by Imagine Dragons," he tells me. He puts the song on repeat, and we listen to it all the way home.

When we get back to the compound, I am almost nervous as to what we're going to find on the other side of the door, but instead, we see everyone over at the banquet hall. I look at Atlas, remembering our skate session and how we had to throw out both chairs, the table, and our clothes to do a deep clean of the place, and I am blushing to my roots. When we get in there, we see dinner is set up.

"It's not Tuesday," Atlas says as we look around at the pinatas and taco table set up. Jaasiel has two eight-foot tables placed together covered in a plastic tablecloth and aluminum foil on top of that with ground beef, chicken, barbacoa beef, steak, birria beef, and pork in the center of the tables. On either side of the meat is lettuce, cheese, tomatoes, onions, jalapeno peppers, cilantro, guacamole, lime, and pico de gallo. There are soft shells, hard shells, and taco bowls, lime-cilantro rice. Margaritas, alcoholic and non-alcoholic, tequila, peach, raspberry, mango, and passionfruit lemonade.

"I felt like tacos," Jaasiel says.

Soon everyone is seated at the dinner table that's been set up, and we are stuffing our faces, laughing and talking. I look around the table, and for the first time in my life, feel like I have a family. I lean over to

Jabarri, "I need your help with something if you don't mind," I whisper to him.

"Find me after dinner, and I'll help you," he tells me with no hesitation.

I nod and find my hand in Atlas' without me remembering reaching for him.

"Did you call the kids and Peter?" Josh asks Savvy.

"I did, they said they'd be here, but maybe something came up."

"Do you want to call them?" he asks.

"No, they know how to get here," she says. "Your problem is you're missing feeling like a father, and you need a fix. And we all know Peter does what he wants."

"I...." he begins when the door opens to all three of Savvy's kids coming in. "Hey, family," they say at the same time.

"Where's my babies?" Atlas asks Saint. They're with their other grandparents.

Atlas rolls his eyes and grumbles.

They head to the restroom to wash their hands and head to the table to make tacos.

A few minutes later, another man walks in. I remember him from the hotel. He walks over to Josh and shakes his hand, and immediately pulls Savvy up from her chair and wraps her in a hug she warmly returns.

"Peter, you have been neglecting me," Savvy says with a pout.

"You know I could never neglect you, little one. I was busy with company business. I am debating on opening an affordable luxury hotel. Your husband is a bad influence on me." Peter says.

He turns to me and says, "Ahh, you must be True. I am Peter the owner of the hotel you were staying at while this guy," throwing his thumb in Atlas' direction, "was being a scared baby."

"I wasn't scared." Atlas' grumbles

"Right, and why was she at my hotel for a month?"

He looks at Atlas with one eyebrow raised.

"I had to work some things out, that's all," he says.

"Scared, you had to go find the balls you misplaced somewhere before you could come get your woman."

"You're an ass, Peter, you know that?" Atlas says.

"Yes, I know, and your point is what? I mean, you're

stating the obvious. Everyone here knows I'm an ass." Peter says with no remorse. As he walks away to wash his hands.

"Is he the one who paid my hotel bill?" I ask Atlas as Peter walks away.

"Yes," Atlas says.

"Oh, I have to give him his money back," I say.

"You will do no such thing. I know you don't know me, but you'll learn quickly. I do not bite my tongue, so if your feelings get hurt easily, don't talk to me. Also, anything I do, I do because I want to, so do not insult me by throwing my gift to you back in my face." He sits across from Savvy with the plate of tacos he made, and I can't help wondering if he's ever had a taco before in his life.

"Jaasiel, these tacos are bussin," Sheppard tells Jaasiel as he gives him a fist bump. He has about eight tacos on two plates. Saint has about the same amount, and much to my surprise, so does Skai.

"Is she going to eat all that," I whisper to Atlas.

"That little walking menace will eat all that and all the food on both her brother's plates too."

"I'm feeling bullied, Uncle Atlas. Uncle Seph, you gonna let him attack me like that?"

"Leave my baby alone, Atlas," Joseph says.

"She's my baby too, and I can mess with her if I want to!"

Joseph's phone chirps before he can respond. He checks his messages and smiles extra wide.

"Who has you smiling like that, Uncle Seph? That pretty woman I saw you with a couple of weeks ago?" she asks. And it's like someone snatched the needle off a playing record. All the attention is on Joseph.

"Excuse me! What woman?" Savvy exclaims.

"Big mouth," Joseph tells Skai.

"Well, you should've gotten me that black-on-black jeep I asked you for," she says around a bite of taco.

"It's in the garage you, brat. You haven't been here for me to give it to you," he grumbles.

"Wait, you actually got it? I was just playing, Uncle Seph," she says, mortified.

"Skai!" Savvy yells at her.

"Momma, I was just playing. I didn't expect him to actually buy it! Who buys someone a car?" she is almost screeching.

"They do!" Savvy says, still yelling. "And you know you can't play with them that way!"

"I'm sorry, Uncle Seph. Can you take it back?" she asks, almost in tears.

"I'm not taking a damn thing back. I bought it for you. And if I didn't want to buy it, I wouldn't have bought it. Skai, the Jeep is yours," he says and kisses her on her temple.

"She is not keeping that Jeep!"

"Baby, relax," Josh tells her.

"So wait, Saint gets a house…

"Leave me out of it." Saint replies.

"And Skai gets a Jeep, what am I chopped liver over here?" Sheppard said on his ninth taco.

"Nah, but I thought you'd like the Trackhawk SRT over a Jeep," Jabarri tells him.

"Y'all planned this?!" Savvy says in confusion.

"Yes, Sheppard and Skai are about to graduate, so this is their early graduation gift from all of us to them. We're proud of you," Josh says.

"You and I are gonna talk about this," Savvy tells Josh. While Skai goes around the table, hugging her uncles and Josh. Sheppard slaps all of them up, grabs another taco, still eating one already, and starts to head out to see his truck. As soon as he gets to the door, Savvy tells him to have a seat. He looks like a toddler that has just been told they can't play with their favorite toy.

Movement catches my attention, and I turn to see Jabarri can't take his eyes off Skai. Once she gets to him, she skips his hug and gets swept up in Atlas' arms. When he puts her back on the floor,

Jabarri asks, "Where's my hug, Skai? I chipped in too."

"How much was your portion?" she asks, and he gives her a figure. She turns and asks Josh for that exact amount. He pulls out his phone and she asks him to transfer it into Jabarri's account instead.

"There's your hug in your bank account," she says.

Before he can respond, the door opens again, and in walks another young lady. I swear I hear Jabarri growl, and Atlas just shakes his head. After the young woman comes back from washing her hands, she speaks to everyone.

"Ms. True, this is Alayna, my girlfriend. Alayna, this is Uncle Atlas' girlfriend." We greet each other, and she digs into the tacos.

"Um, hell no!" Savvy says. "We are not going to ignore the fact that Seph was seen with a woman that none of us knows about. Who is she, Seph, and why haven't we met her?"

"It's not serious, Savvy, that's why. We have an arrangement, nothing more," he says.

"Mmmmhmmm," she says with her lips tooted up.

"Let it go, baby," Josh says. And she sucks her teeth.

Atlas goes back out to the car and grabs the toys we won from the giant mouse, and passes them out to everyone. We hand out slinkies, pinwheels, bouncy balls, candy, pencils, cotton candy, and a bunch of other stuff.

"Tell me you didn't actually go to this kiddie arcade and actually play games to win these prizes," Asher asks, laughing.

"Yes, I did, and I thoroughly enjoyed myself," Atlas says indignantly.

"I think that sounds like a fun afternoon," Savvy says, looking at Atlas with a huge smile on her face.

"GrandPeter!" Skai says, and Peter freezes with his taco halfway to his mouth. He looks down the table at Skai, who's looking at him like she didn't just, in essence, call him her grandfather.

"Yes, baby granddaughter," he replies, and I swear he has tears in his eyes.

"Do you have hotels in Bali? I think Alayna and I want to go there for our graduation trip. But I'm only staying at one of your hotels."

"No but…

"Peter, do not buy a hotel in Bali just so those girls can go vacation there!" Savvy says.

"You don't tell me what to do with my money, Savannah, and I wasn't going to buy a hotel for her! You act like you made my money for me. Skai, you choose any hotel you want to go to, and I will pay for the hotel and all your expenses as a graduation gift. And Sheppard, let me know what you want, and we will work on you getting it. Stop pouting, Savvy. I am allowed to spoil my grandchildren." Peter says as he looks at Savvy, daring her to say her children are not his grandchildren. To my surprise, she doesn't say anything.

We sit in there eating and drinking for a few hours after that, and everyone chips in with the cleaning, and we have the place set to rights in no time. I pull Jabarri to the side and let him know what I need, and he tells me he'll have it ready for me by the next day. He seems pissed, and he has not taken his eyes off Skai. Skai, however, has not bothered to spare him a glance.

"And you!" Josh's voice booms and he gets Jabarri's attention "We're going to talk about that shit!"

I swear I can hear Jabarri swallow. Hell, I'd swallow too. I would hate for all of that attention to be focused on me.

CHAPTER NINETEEN

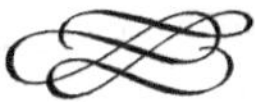

*A*tlas

I put the finishing touches on True's surprise. It wasn't too difficult to keep her in the dark. The woman sleeps like the dead. I have snuck out more times than I can count to handle the Victor situation, and I found her in the same position I left her in. I know she only sleeps like that with me because she feels safe and can let her guard down.

"Baby, aren't you supposed to get your email from the school today letting you know if you were accepted or not?"

"Yes, but I am too nervous to see if it's come and what it says," she says while she nibbles on her thumb.

"Come on, we'll open it together," I say as I steer her towards my desk. I log into my computer. She sits down at the desk and pulls up her email. She scrolls through for a second, and there it is. She hovers the mouse over the email, too afraid to click and open it up, so I lean, place my hand on top of hers, and press the button. The congratulations pops up on the screen, and she screams and slaps her hands over her mouth. Looking up at me with tears in her eyes has me pulling her up into my arms.

"You did it, love. You got in college."

She tries to talk a few times, but she can't. She just shakes her head and holds onto me. I hold her until she calms down.

"I need school supplies. I haven't been to school in years, Atlas. Most of my classes are online, and I don't even have a computer."

"You have time to get all that. I am so proud of you for taking control of your life and figuring out what you want to do with your-self. I will be here to help you every step of the way, and if a teacher fails you, we'll just have Jabarri change it," I tell her, and she slaps my arm and laughs.

"Baby, can you help me decide if I should get a Murphy bed for my third bedroom? I left it empty until I could decide what to do with it."

"Of course," she says as we walk out of our bedroom to the third bedroom.

When she opens the door, the waterworks begin again. I do have a Murphy bed, but I have created an office for her. She has a desktop computer, a laptop computer, an extra-long desk, a few smart note-books, a backpack, pens, pencils, and on and on. "I might have gone a little overboard," I tell her, "but I knew you'd get in, and I was just so proud I couldn't help myself."

"Yes, you did, and I thank you so much for it," she says and kisses me.

We go through the things I bought her and get her logged into her computers. The email has links for her to register for classes and for financial aid, but she pays for it outright. School starts soon, and I know she is nervous. We take our time and plan her schedule and talk about the shelter. We decided to renovate an existing building, and we'll talk to Asher about the remodel once we find the building we want.

"Hello," I bark into the phone.

"We finally got the information on the last shareholder, and we'll be paying him a visit today. I'm sure he'll be willing to sell you his share of the company once he realizes what charges he's being brought up on. We're going to seize all of his other assets, so he'll need the money. Also, Victor's second-in-command was seen arriving in Columbia but has not been seen again. With you taking this last asset from him, I'm sure he'll be coming back to the US to deal with things directly.

"So, in other words, get ready," I say to Doone.

"Get ready," he says, and the line goes dead.

TRUE

It was such an amazing day, learning I was accepted into college, and Atlas surprised me with an office and all the school supplies he bought. I played with my computers and got things set up for school, but beyond that, the shelter is going to become a reality. I searched for the rest of the day, looking for the right location and building. Atlas was helping until he got a phone call, and his whole mood changed. It had to be about Victor. That is the only subject that brings out that side of him. He wouldn't tell me what the conversation was about, and he still hasn't told me why he wants to kill Victor. I want to know, but I do not want to push him. Honestly, when it comes to Victor, it could be anything literally. Even hearing about the things he has done to other people, young girls, and some of the people who work for him is enough to mark him for death. He is a sorry excuse for a human being and a complete psychopath.

Savvy came with me today to look at a couple of properties, and as usual, it has turned into a whole event because Savvy is well Savvy. We have looked at several buildings and locations, and she has brought up some valid points I did not think of. I think Atlas gave her a list of things to ask or look for. We have one more property to look at. If this property is not feasible, we'll have to reconsider building instead. This property is further out than the other properties we have seen today, and it sits by itself.

"I like that this is mostly isolated and on flat ground. The women, men, and children that come here are most likely running and will feel safer without a lot of other people and businesses around." I think out loud to Savvy.

"That's probably true. Are you going to house the men in the same building as the women? That might bother the women and the men if they have been abused by women," she says.

"That's a valid point, and that is why I wanted to house them separately from the women and the family units will be separated as well. It'll be a huge undertaking, but I think if we do it correctly, it will work for everyone," I say my mind is spinning with possibilities.

"Well let me be the first to volunteer my teaching services for the children and even the adults who may need help with reading, writing, or even putting together a resume so they can find work," Savvy offers.

"Thank you for that. That would be amazing and needed. I like this property, there are a few things that would need to be done to get the property to what I need, but I really think this will work." I say.

"You can also purchase the surrounding land if you are interested in that," Blake tells me.

"I'm definitely interested in this property. I just need to let Atlas know so he can come to take a look, too, and then we can go from there." I tell him. We end the property tour with a promise to give Blake a call in a few days. Savvy and I headed back into town to pick up a few things she needed.

"I am so sick of Jag and the brothers using all my hair products!" Savannah says. "Jag used my products one time and claimed his hair was softer and more manageable. He sounded like a damn commercial. Then he had the nerve to give my products to Atlas and Seph to use, and the rest is history. They usually have their own, but if they run out, they come to steal my stash. They do give me money to replace what they use, but do you know how irritating it is to be washing your hair and reach for something to realize you're out because a bunch of grown-ass men has used it all?" she says, shaking her head. "Stop laughing, True, it's not funny."

"I'm sorry, but it is a little funny. Why don't you have Josh contact them and order in bulk? I mean, the amount of hair in that household would need an entire hair store to keep up."

"So true, and maybe I will. I don't know why I didn't think of that. The creator of the line is supposed to be coming out with a new line and I cannot wait to try it. Everything she has created that I've used, I have loved, and she's priced them affordably. But this new line that she released, Melaninque, is her platinum line, and it is double the cost of her other products, and I stay buying the whole line. I am on the verge of contacting them to see if I can buy the products on a buyer's level," Savvy says.

"Well, I'll have to put my name on the list for access to the products too. Once Atlas used them on my hair, that's all I've been using too," I say, smiling at Savvy. "It works wonders on my hair!"

"Well, that explains why Atlas has been stealing twice as much from me. What I don't understand is why they just don't go buy their own instead of always taking from me," she grouses.

"Because you are their sister, and they know you will take care of them, and as much as you talk shit, you love doing it for them.

If you really didn't want to do it or if taking your products was that big of an issue for you, you would have shut it down or had Joshua shut it down," I tell her.

"You don't know me," she says. "And how dare you expose me like that. Don't let them know I enjoy taking care of them."

"Um, I'm pretty sure they already know," I say, laughing.

We get to the store, and she damn near wipes the entire section out. We look around at some other stuff too. In true Savvy fashion, she picks it up and puts it down, grabs a bunch of stuff, adds it up, complains about the cost, and puts it all back. She is hilarious.

If you didn't know her, you would never guess she is married to a multibillionaire. As I am following her, my senses go on full alert. I had this feeling while we were driving from the last property, but it faded when we got to the store. Now it's back in full force. I take a look around but nothing seems out of place. No one sticks out. Savvy finally buys just the hair products.

We stop at a few other stores on our way back to the car but the feeling never leaves. Savvy wants to grab a caramel iced coffee, so we decide to walk to the coffee shop.

"True?" she asks.

"Yep," I reply.

"They have been following us since we left the last property. I wasn't sure, but once we put the bags in the car and began walking and

I saw them again, I was sure," she says calmly, like we are talking about the pastries we are going to get.

"When we get to the next corner we turn and go into the first store she says."

We turn at the corner and go into the first store. We hide to make sure the two men following us come all the way into the store. Once they do, we come up behind them with guns drawn.

"Looking for us?" Savvy asks the guy.

He goes to move, and Savvy takes the safety off.

"I wouldn't do that if I were you. I have no problems shooting your ass right where you stand. Both of you give me your guns." I have the gun Atlas gave me that morning trained on the other guy. They look around to assess their situation.

"Oh, trust me, the scene we'd cause would be Oscar-worthy, so my killing you to defend myself will be justifiable".

Realizing they are stuck they both hand over their guns which Savvy puts in her purse.

"Let's go for a walk," Savvy says and if you act an ass, Brianna, she lifts the gun higher, "will act a bigger ass. Oh, by the way, say cheese," she says as she takes a picture of both men with her phone. She waves the gun and we walk out of the store. Savvy wraps her arm around the guy's arm and holds the gun to his ribs as we walk, and I do the same. To anyone looking at us, we look like two couples shopping. We reach the coffee shop and order our coffee and pastries. As soon as we sit down, Savvy's phone rings.

"Savannah, who the fuck are you with?" the voice bellows over the phone.

"A couple of guys who were following True and I, we're having a nice cup of coffee at Joe Momma Coffee Shop."

"We're on our way," and the phone hangs up.

"Drink up, gentlemen. This might be your last cup of coffee," Savannah says with a smirk.

CHAPTER TWENTY

tlas

Fuck, fuck fuck! I scream. I am well and truly out of time if this has anything to do with True. There isn't a damn thing I will be able to tell Josh. This shit is not good, not just because Savannah is caught in the crossfire but because this can put my family at risk and expose my role in Victor's downfall. One of the main reasons I have been able to get away with all the shit I've been up to is because I'm a ghost, and you can't fight a ghost no matter how powerful you are. I'm hoping like hell this doesn't have anything to do with True but in my gut I know it's a futile wish. Josh broke every speed limit and traffic law known to man to get to his wife in less than 10 minutes, and I know he is reliving her abduction. FUCK! This is a shit storm.

Exactly seven minutes and thirty-nine seconds later, we made it to the coffee shop. All eight of us walk in, and Josh makes an immediate beeline to his wife. I swear that man has a psychic connection with that woman. How did he find her that fast in this crowded coffee shop?

We all pulled up chairs to the small table, and if the situation wasn't so serious, I would've laughed at the looks on the two dead men's faces.

"Who the fuck are you, and why were you following my wife?"

Josh asks with no warm-up. He is not in the mood to play with these men. The man closest to Savvy visibly and audibly swallows.

"We weren't following your wife," the guy stutters out. "We were following her."

He jerks his head in True's direction.

"Why?" Josh asks, and his voice sounds like thunder in an electrical storm. The coffee shop falls so silent you could hear a mouse piss on cotton. Joseph gets up and goes to the counter. Less than five minutes, later the shop is empty, and the closed sign is on the door.

When he comes back over I ask, "How did you manage that?"

"I bought the place," he says with a straight face. I just blink at him.

"Now answer the damn question," Joshua snaps.

"There is a reward for any information on a missing woman matching her description," the guy says. "We were following her to make sure she was the woman we're looking for."

"How much is the reward?" I ask.

"One million dollars," he says.

"Damn," Savvy says, "just for information?" The man just nods like a bobblehead doll.

"Let's go!" Josh says and the chair scrapes across the floor and slams on the floor as it tumbles over. He's pissed, and I can't blame him.

"Aryan, go get Savannah's car," he says as he hands him the keys Savvy gave him.

"Joseph, get our car." We begin walking to the front of the shop. Once outside, Joseph gets out and locks the shop door. Damn, he really bought the place. We put both guys in the back of the SUV.

"Jabarri, erase all the footage. Savvy, make sure you tell him where y'all went today. Asher, take the women home and stay with them. Joseph, Atlas, and I have some business to attend to. The rest of you go back to the site. We'll see you later at home." And that's why he ran special forces teams when he was in the military.

"Maybe I should go with the women instead," I try, and the look Josh levels on me causes me to take a step back.

"Don't back up now, Atlas. We're going to set this shit straight today."

"Asher, when you get to the house, no one leaves under any circumstances, understood?" he says while looking directly at True.

"Understood," Asher says, and we all go our separate ways. Joshua was so pissed he didn't even kiss Savvy goodbye. FUCK!!!!

WE GET to the garage I use to chop cars, shower, and take care of other business I do not want my brothers to know about. We take the men out and tie them to chairs and go outside to talk.

"Gummy, what the fuck is going on? I left you to do you, hoping you'd come to me when the time is right, but you have been determined to do whatever this is on your own. But this has come to our family's door, and that shit is unacceptable. So talk!"

"Joshua, I know I have no right to ask this, and you have no reason to give it to me, but I need a favor."

"A favor?"

"Yes, give me two weeks. Two weeks and we will sit down, and I will tell you everything. Please, Josh, I have never asked for anything, but I am asking for this and for you to let me handle this," I say as I jerk my head toward the garage.

"You're asking for a lot, Gummy," he pulls me in for a hug. "Be careful," he says as he heads back to the SUV, gets in, and pulls off.

I waste no time with niceties and get right down to business. They were after True so they could collect on the reward. Several hours later, I am walking into the house. The guys who were crazy enough to follow True and Savvy, well, let's just say they will never be seen or heard from again. I head directly to my room to find True waiting for me. She does not ask any questions. She's been around this enough. I take a shower, I am exhausted mentally and physically, and now I am on a time clock because Joshua is not going to let me slide with those two weeks. I move to get out of bed, and the phone rings.

"Yeah."

"He'll be back in the States in the next twenty-four to forty-eight hours. He's hired mercs to guard him, so I wouldn't go in alone. There are about twenty to thirty mercs coming with him.

"Understood," I say and hang up the phone.

I hand Anson to Asher. "You have to get them to Uncle Hemi's and get help," I tell him once we are at the halfway point to our aunt and uncle's house.

"Atlas, I'm scared. I can't get them there by myself. You have to come with me and help me!" Asher says damn near in hysterics.

"Ash, you are almost there, just go straight, and you'll be there in no time. I'm going back to help Dad." I tell him.

"He told you not to go back. you promised him you wouldn't come back."

"He needs help, Ash, and I'm the oldest, so it's my responsibility. You're responsible for getting our baby brothers to our aunt and uncle's house as the second oldest," I tell him. He looks at me with tears in his eyes, takes Aryan's hands and starts towards Uncle Hemi' and Aunt Bria's house. I stand there and watch them for a few seconds before I turn back to go back home. I break out in a run, I know my dad is going to be upset but I have to help him. As I get closer to the house, I can hear yelling and my mom screaming for help, and I wonder where my dad is. I finally reach the door. I extend my hand out and grip the knob and......

"Atlas! Atlas, baby wake up! Please wake up! It's just a dream, baby. Please wake up."

I awake with a start, and my face wet with tears. I look at True, and she's crying too. I grab her and hold her so tight she tells me she cannot breathe. She has become my port in a storm without even trying to.

"How long were you trying to wake me up?" I ask her, my voice hoarse.

"I don't know, a while. You were yelling and crying, and I was scared out of my mind. I was just about to go get one of your brothers.

I'm glad she didn't go get one of them. They think the nightmares stopped years ago.

"I'm okay," I lie, my heart is racing and my hands are shaking like a junkie.

"Atlas, can't you tell me why you are having nightmares and why you want to kill Victor? Are they connected? She looks at me with pleading in her eyes but also love and support. She took a chance and told me her past, and no matter what happens, I will never love another woman but True.

"One night, when I was ten years old, my father came into my room with my brother and woke me up. I don't know exactly what time it was, all I knew was it was dark outside. He opened my bedroom window and set us outside with the blanket off my bed, and told us to go to our aunt and uncle's house. He knew our aunt and uncle would be home and would take care of us, but he also knew my uncle would come down to his house, guns blazing." By this time, I am leaning against the headboard and True is sitting crossed-legged in front of me, holding my hands. "He looked at us standing outside the bedroom window and told us he loved us. He also made me promise not to come back to the house. My brothers and I took off to our aunt and uncle's house as fast as our little legs would carry us. Halfway there, I handed Anson to Asher and told him to get them to the house. Asher begged me to come with him, to help him get our brothers to the house. He reminded me that I promised our father that I would not come back. I told him that as the oldest, it was my responsibility to help our father. After a little convincing, he finally took our brother to get to safety and to get help. I watched them for a little while but eventually turned back to our house. I could hear yelling and my mom begging and asking for help. I couldn't figure out where my dad was. I know that if he was there, my mom would not be begging for help. We lived in a pretty big house by ourselves on about an acre or so of land, so there weren't any neighbors to hear or help. I made it to the door and grabbed the knob to open the door, but it just swung open on its own. I went into the kitchen to try to call the police, but the phone wasn't working. I grabbed one of my mom's large kitchen knives and I followed the noises to my parents' bedroom. I tried to stay quiet and out of sight. When I got close enough, I realized the door was ajar, and I could see my mother on the bed bloody and crying, and there was a guy standing next to the bed.

I ran into the room with the knife raised and stabbed him in the thigh. He backhanded me so hard blood exploded from everywhere on my face, and I landed on my back on the floor. He took the blade out of his thigh, came over to me, and cut me across my face from the temple on one side of my face to the neck on the other side. I never knew pain like that existed until I was laying on my parents' bedroom floor, holding my face together as I bled out. As I lay there on the floor, I finally saw my father tied to a chair facing the bed and six guys in the room. My father was missing most of his fingers, his arm was hanging in an unnatural position, one of his eyes was missing, and both his legs were bleeding from what I now know were gunshot wounds. My mother had been raped and beaten by all the men that were in the bedroom. They didn't pay much attention to me. I guess they were just going to let me lay there and die. My father couldn't even speak. He was dying right before my eyes. He eventually locked eyes with me, hurt, worried, but also pissed. I made a promise to him in that very moment I would live, and I would kill every last person who was involved with this. In the middle of all this one of the guys got a phone call, and I knew it was their boss they were talking to. They lied and said they killed everyone. They looked for my brothers, but of course, they were long gone, and I guess they figured we were kids so what were the odds of any of us coming after them? He was pissed because he wanted to use my mom as a way to transport his drugs around the US.

My family's money comes from the steel industry, and we trucked the steel all around the country, and their boss wanted to use our trucks to move his drugs. I found out that night that my mother had an affair, and they were using this affair to try to pressure her compliance. At first, she agreed, but then she decided this was her children's legacy and her sister's and her children's legacy, and she would not jeopardize it. She told this boss she would not allow him to use her company as a way to transport his drugs. She told him she was going to tell my father about the affair, effectively eliminating the leverage he was using against her. My father was supposed to be on a business trip the night the men came to our house, but my mom was really sick that morning and he postponed the trip to help take care of her and us. The men did not expect my father to be home, and he killed three of them before they got the upper hand on him. They were supposed to scare my mother into compliance, but my dad fucked their plans up. When the boss called, they told him my father had killed the three, so they killed all of us. My mother was sick because she was pregnant again and had just told my father that day. She also told him about the affair. Little did she know he already knew and had forgiven her a long time ago. So much miscommunication. Had she not been afraid of my father leaving her, she would have come to him and told him about the blackmail and had my father told her he knew, he would have never had any leverage to use against my mother. I laid there on that floor listening to all of this, listening to my mother being raped repeatedly, with my little sister inside of her, and my father witnessing this and not being able to help. My mother eventually stopped fighting and begging and just resigned herself to death, and my father held on until he watched my mother take her last breath and he took his at the same time. I laid there on that floor and fought for life, I fought for my parents and my brothers who would not grow up with our parents, and I fought for vengeance, for a reckoning. By the time Uncle Hemi made it to the house, both my parents were dead, and I was hanging on by a thread. They rushed me to the hospital and directly into surgery. They told my aunt and uncle my survival didn't look good, but I knew beyond a shadow of a doubt I was going to make it. I was in a medically induced coma for a little while and had a barrage of plastic surgeries to try to fix my face. After the fourth one, I told my Aunt Bria I did not want any more surgeries. My aunt and uncle took us in, and I went from having three brothers to having seven. They never treated us differently. I was truly loved not just by them but by cousins,

Joshua, Joseph, Jaasiel, and Jabarri. I was an angry child. I acted out, got pissy drunk, dabbled in drugs, and attempted suicide more times than I could count. Josh left for the military two years after we moved in, and Joseph left a year later, and that made me angrier. Aunt Bria called Josh home after a series of suicide attempts, drunken stupors, and drug benders, and he got in my ass. He walked in on another attempt, and he read me the riot act. I pulled it together and remembered the promise I gave to my father to eliminate every piece of shit involved in his and my mother's death. My childhood ended in that bedroom that night, and my adulthood started the day Joshua told me to get my shit together.

My brothers never knew what happened. I told them I didn't remember. And all I had to go off of was the names they called each other in that room and their faces. I would NEVER forget those faces. I went into the military to gain skills, I went into the DEA to gain access, and I hunted my whole life to get to the guy who orchestrated my parent's death and the destruction of my family. A few months ago, I got that name…. Victor. The night I found you, I was going to finally kill the man who killed my family, but I found you instead. He is on his way back from Columbia, and I plan on being there at the compound to finally put this shit behind me. Doone called and said he'd be back in the states in a couple of days, and I plan on having a welcome home gift when he touches down. He's killed so many of his men, or they have defected until he has had to hire around twenty to thirty mercs to protect him.

TRUE

I sit there holding Atlas' hands, speechless, with tears free-flowing down my face. I cry for the little boy who should have never had to lose his parents and the man that has been carrying that around all his life. I knew whatever it was, was going to be fucked up, but I would have never guessed it was going to be this fucked up. "Atlas, you can't go up against that many mercs by yourself, and you don't know if he has any more help here. Even if we go together, we probably won't make it out alive. I understand how you feel, probably better than anyone. I mean, after all, he's the reason my mother is dead, I'm sterile, and I grew up fucked up. But maybe it's time we let this vendetta go. I found a love in you I would have never dreamed possible. I have done more with you and lived more in the few months we have been together than I have in my entire life. Maybe it's time we put the past behind us and move forward. If he's had to hire mercs, I take it you have dismantled his organization. There were nights I woke up to find you gone, but you were always back by morning. Please, Atlas, let this go, and let you and I move into our future together." I beg him.

"You expect me to not kill Victor after what I just told you he caused to happen to my family? After I have worked all my life to take his ass down? After all the money, blood, sweat, and tears I have given? I've loved the time we have spent together and all the experiences we have had together that I should have had in my youth, but there is no way I could walk away after getting this close to fulfilling the promise I made to my father." He looks at me like I told him the sun rotates around the earth.

"Atlas, please, I don't want to lose you, and I am not ready to die. At least let your brothers help. I know with them, we'd all make it out alive." I am on my knees, holding his face in my hands, begging him not to do this.

"I do not want my brothers involved with this, True. I would not make it if I lost another person I love. You have to promise me not to tell my brothers anything," he says, grabbing my upper arms in a bruising grip. I wince, and he lets me go. "I do not want you coming with me either. I wouldn't survive if you got hurt or were killed. I want you to stay here at the compound with my brothers."

"Atlas, I will not wait here to see if you come back to me. If you don't let this go I am not going to be here when you get back," I say in a last-ditch effort to get him to change his mind. I am hoping he doesn't call my bluff because I don't think I could function without him.

"True, don't give me this ultimatum. You are not going to like the outcome. As much as I love you, and I know I will never love anyone else if you leave me, but I will not let this go. I will see this through, even if it costs me my life," he says with steel laced in his voice.

"If you don't let this go and put the past behind us, I

will not be here when you get back. I love you too, but I cannot bury you, I won't do it!" I scramble off the bed.

"You don't have much faith in me, True. What makes you think I am going to die?" he asks me.

"The thirty fucking mercs, Atlas! You won't let your brothers help or let me help, and you are going into Victor's compound alone to face thirty or more hired mercenaries. I won't sit here and wait for you to die! Why can't you let this go and come live with me instead."

"YOU KNOW WHY!" he screams in my face. "Why can't you support me? Why can't you wait for me? Understand why I must do this? I'm going, True, and I hope that WHEN I get back, I will find you here. But if I don't, I'll learn to live without you," he says as he damn near rips the door off the hinges as he storms out of the room. I want to throw myself on the bed and cry like the female lead in a 1940s movie. I don't throw myself on the bed, but I do cry like a baby.

CHAPTER TWENTY ONE

Atlas

I'm lying my ass off. I know good and damn well I will not give True up. No matter what. I will go take care of this Victor situation, and then I will come back, and True and I will work through this and put it behind us. I go downstairs to ask for one more favor, and I hope he doesn't ask too many questions. I knock on their door and wait for them to tell me to come in. The last time I walked in without knocking, Josh almost knocked my ass out, seeing that Savvy was walking naked out of the shower. I hadn't gotten used to her being here and was used to just walking in and talking to my brother. Luckily for me, I did not see anything, and I hustled my ass out of there before I was missing one or both of my eyes. Come in! I hear Josh bellow. The door quietly swings open, and I walk down the hall to their living room and have to pick my jaw up off the ground at the sight that greets me.

My seven-foot, three-hundred-and-fifty-pound brother is reclining in his seat with an Aztec clay face mask on his face with cucumber slices over his eyes while Savvy is giving him a manicure. I look down at his feet that he has propped up on a footrest, and his toes are painted the same bubble gum pink as Savannah's toes. I blink, then blink again because I cannot be seeing what I am seeing.

"You better have a damn good reason for disturbing my spa time, Atlas," he says, and my eyebrows touch my hairline. I stand there dumbfounded and truly cannot find any words to say. He eventually reaches up and plucks both cucumber slices off his eyes and looks at me. I'm still standing there, blinking at this scene. "Say what you want, or get the hell out," he barks at me, and finally, I snap out of it.

"Um, I, I need your help," I stutter out.

Now it's time for his eyebrows to touch his hairline, "Help? What kind of help?" he asks.

"I need Savvy to keep True here." At this point, Josh sits all the way up. Savvy gets up and goes over to make her and Josh some tea. Tea is her favorite drink outside of her peach lemonade. She drinks it by the gallons, especially when she's writing. When he saw her using two different flavors of tea bags to get the flavor she wanted, in true Joshua fashion, he had a blend created and named after her. Not to be outdone, Savvy went and had a custom blend made for him, and is also named after him.

"Give me a minute," he says and walks down the hall. When he returns, he has washed the face mask off, and I swear his skin is glowing.

"Is your skin glowing?" I ask him.

"You can kiss my ass," he returns.

"Why is Savvy keeping True here?" he says as he takes the cup of tea from her, and she sits next to him.

"We kinda got into a discussion, and she's threatened to leave, and I need to leave to handle some business so I would feel better knowing that she's here so we can work this out when I get back," I say, leaving out…...everything.

"What was the argument about that would make her threaten to leave you?" Savvy asks.

"You can't ask what we argued about. I don't want to get into it right now."

"Wrong," he says instantly. "I'm going to ask all the damn questions when it comes to asking my wife to keep a person held against their will!"

"Jag, baby, let him talk," Savvy says before he can get more wound up.

And just like that he sits back and snaps, "Talk!"

"Could you give Savannah up under any circumstances?"

"Don't be ridiculous, Atlas," he growls out. "I would never do anything so stupid."

"Well, I feel the same way about True. I would do almost anything to keep her. Tempers flared, and we both said some things we didn't mean. I just don't want her to run off before we get the chance to talk again."

"And what business do you need to attend to that's so important you can't work things out with True first?" Josh asks, looking straight through me.

I just look at him. After a second, he realizes I'm not going to answer, and he just grunts. The tea mug clatters as he sets it down because what he's drinking out of can in no way be considered a teacup, and stands to his full height and walks over to me so close we are practically touching chest to chest. He looks me in my eyes and says, "Please do not put me in the position of having to bury your ass because something has happened to Savannah behind your bullshit. I love you both, but she is my greatest treasure, and if I was to lose her, I would not go on living. Not that I wouldn't want to, I would simply stop existing without her. She is my beating heart and my immortal soul. But make no mistake, I would annihilate your ass before I go into the afterlife with her." He looks me dead in the eyes, ten toes down, and says this with truth burning in his eyes, and I completely believe him.

For a second, I falter, I do not want anything to happen to Savvy, and I do not want to lose my brother behind it because I believe he would literally die without Savannah, but I need Savvy's help to keep True here. I stand there at a loss again, not knowing what to say to Josh. So I tell him the truth as much as I can.

"I need Savvy's help. I love True the same way you love Savvy, and I do not want anything to happen to either one of them."

He stares at me for a second before he says, "This is getting to be too much for you. Promise me you will come to me. Give me a chance to get Savvy someplace safe."

"I promise," I say with no hesitation. We stare at each other for a few more seconds, understanding passing between the two of us. As I turn to go back to my room, I hear him call out to me.

"Atlas!"

"Yeah?"

"Times up."

Fuck!

I go back to my room once I have ensured True cannot leave me, and I prepare for the war I am getting ready to fight. I plan on taking Victor by surprise. I am sure he would not be expecting me to show up as soon as he gets back to US soil. I plan on blowing up some shit, and that should take out a good majority of the men he's bought with him. When I walk into my bedroom, True is sitting in the same spot I left her in and I can tell she's been crying. I go to her and pull her into my arms, she tries to fight me, but it's a feeble fight she puts up. I hold her to my chest and tell her how much I love her, and I beg her to wait for me. I release her and go to my hidden weapons closet, put the code in, and walk in when the door slides open. I grab my favorite set of knives, my guns, grenades, and the rocket launcher in the weapons locker in the garage. I fill up the duffle bag with all my equipment and change into all-black fatigues. I plan on hitting Victor's house under the cover of night. Once I have all the weapons I want and can carry, I close the closet and set the bag on the bed. True is in the same spot.

"Will you at least give me a kiss before I leave?" I say, reaching out my hand to her.

She hesitates for a few seconds but comes willingly into my arms. I take my time kissing her, pouring all the love I have for her into the kiss. When I break the connection, I caress her face and gaze into her eyes.

"Wait for me," I say, turning on my heels and walking out of the room.

I get to the garage, grab the rest of the weapons I need, load everything in the car, and begin the twelve or so hour trip to finish what was started over thirty years ago.

True

I cannot believe he actually left me. I mean, I know giving him an ultimatum was a cowardly move but, I was willing to try anything to keep him here. The odds of him making it back to me without help is slim to none. How do I navigate this world without him in it? Who will take me to the fair, skating, and the kiddie arcades? Who will make me feel like a whole woman even though I know I will never be a mother? He has done more for me than I have done for him. He won't ask for help from his brothers or allow me to help him, stubborn bastard, and he made me promise not to tell his brothers.

It takes a few seconds for me to register the knock on the door.

"Come in!" I yell because I don't have the desire to move from the bed.

"Hey, sis, what's going on?" Savvy asks me, full of concern. "You look like hell."

"Gee, thanks," I reply dryly.

"I call them like I see them. What is going on between you and my brother?

"We're not seeing eye to eye on a subject. He's as stubborn as a mule," I tell her, anger creeping into my voice.

"They are all stubborn. You know that. Was he being unreasonable?"

"Yes!" I say vehemently.

"Unreasonable to you? Or just unreasonable?" she asks me, one eyebrow raised.

"I mean……"

"Aww, unreasonable to you. Loving these brothers is different. They are stubborn jackasses at times, especially when it comes to protecting who they love, but the benefits are so worth it. On the flip side, sometimes they need help and are too unwilling to ask, and you have to step in and take the backlash. Figure out which one this is and do what you gotta do. Get up and get dressed. I'll be back with lunch, Jaasiel cooked." she says with a gleam in her eyes. And I don't blame her. That man can cook his ass off. Why he doesn't have his own restaurant is mind-boggling to me.

Atlas

I am looking at Victor's compound through some high-power binoculars. There are about thirty men that I could see here, and they are heavily armed. True was probably right. I probably won't make it out of this alive, but one thing is for sure Victor's bitch ass is dying too. He has been held up inside the house like the fucking coward he is. Once the sun sets, I am going in. I think of True and even though I might not make it out alive, I do not regret my decision not to let her come with me. I'd rather her and my brothers live even if I die. I love them all that much, and no I am not trying to be a martyr, but I watched two people I loved more than anything else in this world die, and I refuse to bear witness to that again. But I also won't let my parent's death go unanswered. Just a few more hours and this shit will finally be over one way or the other. All I have to do is sit and wait...

Fuck, they have me pinned down and are advancing on me. I get ready to go at them head-on when I hear the sounds of shots being fired and bodies dropping. Once it's quiet, I stand, gun drawn, and see True standing there.

"You're so fucking hard-headed! I told you to stay home, True. what the fuck are you doing here?" I say, equally happy to see her and pissed that she's here. I get it. True is not the sit-at-home and knit type of woman, and I guess I kinda expected her to show up. But if she dies here, I would not be able to live with myself.

"We don't have time for this shit. Let's find Victor, kill him, and get the hell out of here. We can argue at home," she tells me.

Damn, I love this woman. We head further into the house towards Victor's bedroom, where it is guarded the heaviest. A bullet whizzes by us, and we duck for cover.

True lays down on her stomach, takes aim, and begins picking off anyone she can get a bead on. I take out to anyone she can't. The door behind us opens and more men begin to file in. I pull True over to me, using her belt to get her out of the line of fire. There are more men here than I anticipated, and I am glad I have True with me. We crouch down for a couple of seconds. We stand together, back to back, a gun in each hand, and begin shooting. We turn like one person, like we've practiced it a million times. She drops to a crouch, and we spin again. She stands up and we begin moving, spinning, shooting, and moving the whole time, making our way to Victor. We are almost where we need to be when I feel a burning sensation in my chest, and I look down to see liquid seeping through my shirt. Before I can register what happened, I'm hit three more times. My arm, thigh, and side. I drop to one knee holding my sideman the body armor I have on no longer providing protection.

"ATLAS!" True screams. She finds who shot me, a guy we shot but didn't kill is holding the gun that shot me. True empties her clip in the man screaming the whole time. By the time she gets back to me, I am lying flat on my back, struggling to breathe.

"Atlas, baby don't you die on me," she says looking down on me crying. "We're going to make it out of here, together. We still have to kill Victor. You can't die yet. You're not supposed to die until we're old and gray," she's holding my face crying ugly tears, as she calls them. We hear a commotion outside the door. The other men just came through and I lift my gun as best I can just as True turns around, sitting in front of me with both guns drawn. The door opens, and Joshua walks in with Joseph, and I swear I have never seen a more beautiful sight.

"Fuck, Atlas," Josh says as he comes over to me.

"We're going to get into this shit once this is over. Victor must have called in for reinforcements. Your brothers are outside taking care of that. We have to get you out of here to Aryan so he can try to patch your stupid ass up, and we can get you to a hospital."

"No, I'm finishing this tonight!" I tell him. "Just help me up."

"Are you crazy?" Joseph exclaims. "You've been shot four times. You are lying in a puddle of your own blood. We've got to get you out of here."

Before anything else can be said, more guys start coming in, and shooting at us, they're like roaches; they just keep coming. The door behind us opens again and in walks the rest of my brothers, except Aryan. They are cutting a swath through these men with ease.

"We've got to get Atlas out of here!" One of my brothers says. I'm fading, so I can't determine which brother. I feel True pulling on me to sit up, she puts her shoulder under my arm and tells me to get up! I use my hand to push myself off the floor and use her as leverage, but she cannot support me by herself, and my brothers are fighting. Just as I get ready to buckle, I feel someone grab me from the other side and realize it's Savvy. Holy shit Josh let her come? Together we make it outside while Aryan is out there picking off anyone who tries to escape or go in to help. We get to Aryan, and Savannah takes over for him while Aryan works on patching me up. He stops the bleeding with battle dressings and gives me a shot for the pain. As soon as I am patched up to his satisfaction, he takes back over from Savannah. A few seconds later, Aryan heads into the house too. They are communicating with earbuds. Savvy puts one in my ear so I can hear what is going on. Josh tells her to get me to a hospital. They get me up and try to get me to get in the car, but I am finishing this tonight.

"I need to go back in," I tell them. They stand there for a few seconds and just look at me, and I ready myself for the argument I know is coming but instead True says, "Okay."

"I'll stay here. This is between you and True," Savvy says.

True and I make it to the side of the house where Victor's personal door is and walk in unhindered. We make it to Victor's bedroom, but he is not there. We keep going until we find him in his home office.

He is sitting behind his desk, smoking a cigar and drinking what looks like whiskey. He looks up at me and True and blinks, completely unbothered by us being here. The house is quiet, and I hear Joshua in my ear telling me all clear.

"True, you little bitch. I knew you were behind this," Victor says. "How did you convince this guy to help you? Is your pussy so good that this guy would risk death to help you?" he says and laughs. "Your mother's was. it was so good I haven't been able to get over her even after all these years," he glazes over as he remembers True's mother. "When she came back to me with a child, I should have just killed you then, but I couldn't do that to your mother. I couldn't hurt that way. But she left me anyway, ungrateful bitch. So who is this chump?"

"I didn't have to find him, he found me, and we both realized what a public service it would be to wipe your ass and everything you created off the face of the earth," she tells him. "You didn't love my mother. You groomed her and destroyed her, you narcissistic, delusional bastard! She had to kill herself to get away from you.

"Semantics," he says, completely monotone. "And what did I supposedly do to you?" He looks completely bored.

"You killed my parents," I told him. "You destroyed mine and my brothers' world that night."

"Hmm, you're old, so this must have taken place at least thirty years ago. I was just building my empire then. Who were your parents? I do not remember them." He comes around to the front of his desk, leans his butt on the edge, and crosses his ankles. "I want to hear the story. Tell me the story."

And I do. As I tell the story, he listens intently.

"Ah, yes, I remember this. Those idiots told me they killed all of you. Had I known they left any of you alive, I would've come back and killed all of you and the family you were living with too. This is why it is easier to kill everyone you have a problem with, so they don't have the opportunity to come back after you," he says, laughing. "Truthfully, if your stupid useless mother would've just went along with the program, she would be alive today. It's her fault she and your father are dead, not mine. I didn't give her, your father, you, or your brothers a second thought. They were insignificant then, and they are insignificant now." He stands to his full height, and before I can register what he is getting ready to do, he pulls out a gun and shoots True.

As she falls forward, he grabs her and puts the gun to her neck. "I knew this day would come eventually, I did all I could to avoid this shit. Killing all my enemies and their families and not having any children or anything that could and would be held against me. And something that I didn't even order comes back more than thirty years later to bite me in the ass, but if I have to go, True is going with me."

He says as he prepares to shoot True. Our eyes lock, and she pulls a blade from her belt and stabs him in his thigh. He screams in pain but does not let her go. I make a move for him, and he turns the gun on me. True pulls the blade out of his thigh and slices his wrist with it as I grab the gun and release the clip. True finally moves out of his grip. I release his hand, pull my blade and slice him across his abdomen. He takes the hand and hits me on my temple with the butt of the gun, I stagger, and he swings again, but this time he hits True, and she staggers. "You two are both pitiful. You've both wasted over thirty years of your life trying to kill me and where has it gotten you?" he says, laughing, holding his abdomen. "And you still can't kill me, and I am standing right in front of you. Before I can think about it, I take my blade and stab him in the top of his head and True takes her blade and stabs it up through his mouth at the same time. The look in his eyes is almost comical, he is genuinely surprised that we have killed him.

I think, in his delusional mind, he was going to make it out of this alive. We pull our blades out, and his body drops to the ground like a sack of rotten potatoes. I look at him, laying their eyes wide with surprise, and spit on his body. I wish I wasn't hurt because I would have taken hours torturing him. Although I look over at True and know I wouldn't have wasted any more time on him.

"I've spent enough of my life on this sorry piece of shit. Let's go home," I say to True. I reach out to take her hand and everything goes black.

CHAPTER TWENTY TWO

True

"JAG!" I scream as I sit on the floor, holding Atlas as best as I can. I keep screaming, not thinking about the fact that I am calling him Savvy's nickname for him. He bursts through the door with the brothers hot on his heels.

"He collapsed! I can't feel a pulse, and his chest isn't moving. Please help him." I am full-fledged hysterical at this point. Joshua lifts him, and Asher helps him. They rush him out to the chopper. Aryan and I climb in as he barks at the pilot to take off. Aryan begins performing CPR on him as I hold his hand and whisper in his ear how much I love him and how much his brothers love him. I beg him to hold on. As we climb higher, I hear and see an explosion, and I realize they have blown Victor's house up. A few seconds later, the other choppers are in the air, and we are racing to a hospital. I swear if he dies, I will find a way to die just so I can cuss his ass out.

We made it to the hospital. They tried to give us a hard time with us landing on the helipad, and we are not a medical transport. But luckily, Asher called Doone and Doone called the hospital and explained that this was a DEA agent and was coming in hot. Once we landed, the nurse and doctor took over for Aryan. He never stopped the whole ride, he continued to give his brother CPR, and I know he must be exhausted. They took one look at Atlas and rushed him directly into surgery. We sat in the waiting room for hours, waiting on any news of his condition. We are all worried because he never breathed on his own, and he never regained consciousness. His brothers look scared shitless. He has always been their protector and strength, and if he doesn't make it, they'd be lost.

Several hours later, a doctor finally comes out to give us the news that Alas made it through surgery but is far from being out of the woods.

"Make him stable enough to transport to another hospital?" Asher asks.

"I wouldn't recommend moving him right now," the doctor replies.

"I didn't ask you, I said make him stable enough to move." Asher tells the doctor as he towers over him.

"He'll need the proper equipment and a nurse or doctor to monitor him," he says, damn near shaking.

"Make it happen!" Asher snaps.

The doctor scampers away to make the arrangement, and I look at Asher, realizing I have never seen this side of him before. They finally load Atlas up in the medicopter, and Aryan goes with them to keep an eye on his brother. The brothers rented SUVs, and we began our drive to Mississippi. The adrenaline starts to wear off, and I'm fading fast. I crawl into the back seat, lay down, and fall asleep.

Anson wakes me up once we get to the hospital. I pull my head together and head inside. The first person we see as we walk in is Peter.

"I called in a few favors. He is upstairs in a private suite. He has his own nurse specifically for him and a doctor friend of mine to make sure he gets the best care possible. You guys can go on up to the room. Aryan is already up there with him. True, there is a pull-out twin sofa bed in the room for you to stay with him as long as he's here once you get patched up. I will have food delivered for you guys too. I'm going to head home. I'll be back later." Peter pulls Savvy into a hug and then pulls me into a hug, too, and I almost break, but I need to see Atlas.

Once he releases me, he nods at the brothers and walks towards the elevators to go home.

We finally reach the room, and I pause at the door. I am almost too scared to see what is on the other side of the door. Anson grabs my hand, opens the door, and pulls me into the room. My eyes immediately find Atlas laying in the bed, looking more vulnerable than I have ever seen him, and I break down. He looks so small and fragile. The machines are breathing for him, and he has a few IVs in him. He had so many injuries, including a nicked lung and blood loss, and it's left him in a coma. We all settle down in the room and wait. Little by little, the brothers trickle out to head home. Eventually, I find myself alone with Atlas. I scoot the chair next to his bed, grab his hand and begin talking.

"You have brought me so much peace and created a space for me that has allowed me to heal. I am glad I didn't succeed in killing Victor that night. It was meant for us to kill him together. When you left me to go kill him, I shouldn't have hesitated for one second. You are my home, Atlas, you are my family and even though I am incomplete, I am whole with you. You have worked for over thirty years to finally avenge your parents. You deserve this rest and more as long as you wake your ass up ...soon." A bag arrives later with some clothes and toiletries. Savannah must have packed this. Only a woman would be this thorough.

Four weeks Later:

I am still at the hospital. Atlas has not woken up yet. School has started, and I am doing online classes because I refuse to leave him. The doctors have told us that the longer he stays in a coma, the worse his odds are of waking up. I shower, dress, eat, and go to school from this hospital room, I'm not leaving until Atlas and I leave together. Peter has had food brought here every day just like he said he would, and Savvy comes every day to sit with Atlas and me and to take my clothes to wash them and bring me fresh clothes. All the brothers come every day without fail. One day I was sitting reading a novel to him, and the door swung open with a bang, and in walks Skai.

She runs over to the bed with tears in her eyes. "Uncle Atlas, you have to wake up. I need you at my graduation ceremony," she's damn near climbing in the bed, crying over Atlas.

The only improvement we've seen is him being taken off the ventilator for him to breathe on his own. But other than that, no change in his condition. I walk out of the bathroom after taking a shower and the room is full with the brothers and Savannah.

"Is it family night?" I ask.

"Yep, I had Atlas' favorite restaurant in New Orleans gumbo brought in," Josh says.

"I hope you have a bowl for me," Atlas says. And I almost collapsed with relief.

"Where are you, baby? he says, looking for me. I rush to the side of the bed, grabbing the pitcher of ice water to pour him a cup. I place the straw to his lips, and he takes a couple of sips of water before saying "I've been fighting to get back to you to ask you something."

"You can ask me anything," I tell him.

"Will you allow me to be your husband? I don't have a ring right now, but as soon as I blow this popsicle stand you can go pick out whatever ring you want. I mean, if you say yes, that is," he looks so much lighter even though he still has a long road of recovery ahead of him. "I'll even go get my face fixed."

"Yes, Atlas. I would love for you to be my husband. I'd be honored and your face is perfect. Don't you dare change it," I say in tears.

"Well, your ass better hurry up and get better cause we gonna get into this shit!" Josh bellows.

"Damn baby, he just woke up. You have plenty of time to fuck him up for being a reckless jackass and scaring us to death," Savvy says.

"Atlas, what happened?" Anson says so quietly it's barely audible.

Atlas

I can hear the voices of my family, and I once again try to break through the darkness to get back to them. I have listened to all of them on and off for I don't know how long, but it's True's voice that I have heard consistently begging me to come back to her. She goes from begging me to cussing me out to crying, and through it all I am fighting to get to her. I am so tired, and everything hurts. There are times I wanna say fuck it and just let go. Today is one of those days. I am tired, in pain, and I fulfilled the promise I made more than thirty years ago. I begin to loosen the hold on the tether that is keeping me here and slip deeper into the darkness. I find myself in a hallway with a door at the end and begin walking toward it. I reach my hand out to grasp the knob to open the door and walk into whatever is awaiting me on the other side. As soon as my hand touches the smooth metal, a large rough hand covers mine. I'd know that hand from anywhere even though I haven't felt it touch my skin in thirty-eight years. I remove my hand and slowly turn to look into the emerald-green eyes of my father. "Da," I say as I embrace him in a bone-crushing embrace. Once we release each other, my father grabs my face and just looks at me.

"Atlas, look at you! You've become a fine young man! I am so sorry I missed so much of your and your brother's lives. I'm sorry I could not be stronger for you, your brothers, and your mother. I let you all down, and you've had to live with my failure.

But you still have life left to live and a woman that walked into hell with you and walked out by your side. Let it go now, Atlas, and go back to our family. This burden was never yours to carry, so go live. You made me a promise that night we were all dying in that room, and now I want you to make me another one," Da says.

"What promise, Da?" I ask him.

"That you will fight to get back our family and live this life until there is nothing left to live. When it's time for you to leave this life, I want you to be ready for you to walk into death's arms with a smile and not with regret. Now is not your time. Your mother, sister, and I will be here when it is your time, but not now."

"Sister?"

"Yes, her name is Alexandria. Open the door," my dad says to me. I grasp the knob again, and this time the door opens. Standing there in the most beautiful field is my mother, her auburn hair flowing around her shoulders, holding my baby sister with a mop of red hair of her own. I try to walk to them, but I cannot make it past the threshold. My father walks around in front of me. "It's not your time yet, son. You cannot cross over. Go back to your brothers and your woman. We'll see you soon enough," he says as he embraces me again, I hold onto him, recalling all the years I missed his embrace, smile, and voice. We release each other at the same time, and he walks to my mother and sister's side and wraps his arms around them. I stand there looking at them until the door closes and I am being pulled, but instead of giving up like I was doing, I fight to push through the darkness to get back to my family, my future.

I can hear Savvy talking about gumbo, but I do not hear True's voice, and I swear I can smell the gumbo. Finally, I break through the darkness, through the fog I have been surrounded by.

"I hope you have a bowl for me." I croak out. Although I haven't heard True's voice, I know she is there. "Where are you, baby? I say a little stronger. I finally see the most beautiful sight outside of just seeing my parents and sister as she places a straw to my lips. I take a few deep sips of the cool liquid. Before I could lose my nerve or consciousness, I ask her to marry me, and she says yes. She damn near cusses me out when I suggest fixing my face. And then I hear my baby brother ask me what happened, and I realize I do not know how they knew where to find me. I assume it was True even though she promised me she wouldn't, but how can I be mad at her when she's the reason I am still alive. I open my mouth to answer my brother when the nurses come into the room. For the next few hours, I am poked and prodded within an inch of my life.

Once they are done running tests and evaluating me, they finally leave me alone with my family. I had a few sips of broth from the gumbo. I didn't want to chance eating more. I look around the room at my brothers. "I never told you what happened the night our parents were killed," I say to Anson. "I made a promise that night as I lay on the floor and bled out as my face was sliced open. I promised our father that I would avenge their deaths. I lied to you all these years about not remembering what happened, and I never told the authorities what really happened. I wanted to find the people responsible for the destruction of our family myself. After the last time, I tried to unalive myself, and Joshua came and talked some sense into me, I focused my life on avenging our parents' death," I say. I go into the truth of the night that changed our lives forever. When I am done with what happened that night, I want answers myself. "I take it True told you where to find us," I say. "Even though she promised not to tell y'all."

"Actually, she told me," Savvy said, "and as far as I know, you didn't make her promise not to tell me."

"When Savvy came up to the room to talk to me and keep an eye on me, I decided I really didn't give a damn what you said. I was coming to help you, and we'd figure it out after we made it out alive. Cause I would rather have you mad at me alive than okay with me and dead. After she left the room I ...."

And True begins to tell me how she ended up coming to my rescue.

True & Savvy:

"Loving these brothers is different. They are stubborn jackasses at times, especially when it comes to protecting who they love, but the benefits are so worth it. On the flip side, sometimes they need help and are too unwilling to ask, and you have to step in and take the backlash. Figure out which one this is and do what you gotta do. Get up and get dressed. I'll be back with lunch, Jaasiel cooked." she says with a gleam in her eyes. And I don't blame her. That man can cook his ass off. Why he doesn't have his own restaurant is mind-boggling to me.

Savvy walks out of the room, and I really think about her words, and I'm gonna go with option B. I jump up and head to the bathroom. I shower in record time and get dressed. All black seems appropriate.

I head to Atlas' hidden weapons closet and put the code in. Yeah, I watched when he put the code in, so sue me. I grab a backpack and load it up with handguns, knives, and some explosives. If Savvy came to see what was going on, that could only mean Atlas went to them, and since I know he didn't tell them what was really going on because they'd all be going after him, he had to talk to them about something else. Probably asked Savvy to keep an eye on me, but since they don't know the seriousness of the situation, I am sure they are not going to watch me too closely. I took the same route we took the night of the skate date, and we had to sneak in Butterball naked, thanks to Atlas cutting our clothes off.

I make it to the garage to load Atlas' NSX because it's fast, and I am hours behind him and take off to Victor's compound. I am not even close to driving the speed limit, but I am keeping an eye out for police because I cannot afford to get pulled over. I didn't take the back roads like Atlas does. I don't have time for that shit; I am already behind. The closer I get, the more my stomach turns to stone. Why did I make that stupid ass decision not to tell his brothers? We need their help. Savvy's words really hit home. Once she left, I realized that fuck this life if I couldn't live it with Atlas. He is worth it, he's worth every-thing, and I'll be damned if I sit here like a wilting violet while he goes off to get killed. I'm coming to help cause I'd rather he be mad at me and alive, than dead. So fuck that. If he dies, we die. We're going to do that shit together but we're going to put up a hell of a fight before we just *let* it happen. We need his brother's help. Do I break my promise to him? Why not? I'm already going against his wishes, in for a penny and all that. I activate the phone when it hits. I do not have any of the brothers' numbers, and Atlas does not have them programmed into the car.

"Fuck!" Wait, I think, as a slow smile creeps across my face. I do have Savannah's phone number.

"Where the hell are you?!" she yells as soon as she answers.

"Savvy, I need you to listen. This is important," I tell her, cutting off her rant. I tell her everything that happened, including the argu-ment and my ultimatum. I tell her Atlas has left to get himself killed and that I am on my way to help him, but we are going to need help. I can hear her yelling for Josh and telling him what I am telling her.

"Where are you? Jabarri couldn't track you guys," she asks in a rush.

"I am almost to the compound in Texas," giving her the address.

"Atlas is already here fighting by himself. We are going to need your help. Please hurry," I say and hang up.

My nerves are so bad, and I turn the radio on to try to calm them. These last thirty minutes are taking so long, and I am struggling to keep my composure. The music comes on, and I zone out as I push it to get there. I tune back in as the words to a particular song penetrate my mental meltdown. As I listen, a particularly determined tear slides down my face, and once that one drops, the rest follow. As Andy Grammer sings about not giving up, I feel the words down to my bones because I refuse to give up on Atlas. I make it to the compound and park where Atlas parked his SUV that fateful night when he saved my life. It's like World War 3 here, and I am surprised there are no cops on the way, but then again, he probably owns the cops, plus his compound is pretty isolated. I get out of the car and strap up with a gun on each thigh and hip and one at the small of my back. My weapons belt holds extra ammo, clips, and a few knives. I stuff a few grenades anywhere they can fit and head in to find Atlas.

Savvy

"Go get my brother, Joshua!" I'm yelling at him in near hysteria.

"Savannah, calm down, we are going to help Atlas, and once we get him out of this mess, I am going to kill him myself. I told him on repeat, to come to me when he was ready, not to try to do this by himself. He is so fucking stubborn and hardheaded. What are you doing, Savvy?" he asks me.

"If you think I am going to sit in this house and wait for you like a good little girl, you are sadly mistaken, Joshua Abraham Gideon! Now how are we getting to Texas fast enough to help my brother?"

"You say it like he's not my brother too, Savannah," he whirls around and tells me. He grabs my face and looks into my eyes,

"I know you are scared and so am I, but Atlas is a tough son of a bitch. He'll hang on until we get there, baby. He won't die. We'll get to him. Are you ready to go?" he asked me.

"Yes," I say, smiling because he has never tried to harness me, and he understood that I needed to come with them and didn't fight me on it. "But how are we getting …." I never finish my statement due to the sound of the helicopter, scratch that helicopter's landing. When we walk out to get in the chopper, Jag and his seven brothers look like every branch of every armed force on the planet. They are some dangerous-looking mother fuckers. We head out of the house and load up in the chopper, and head to Texas.

"And all that lead us here," True says as she lies in bed with me.

EPILOGUE

TRUE

*H*aving no family should have made this wedding weird or lonely, but I forget that I do, in fact, have a family. Savannah, Skai, Aalayna, Shell, Bailey, and Megan show up and help me get dressed. Atlas refused to wait more than a month for us to get married. Luckily for us, the venue was already built so it was a matter of finding dresses. I chose a navy-blue dress because that is Atlas' favorite color. The girls wore gold dresses, Atlas wore a navy tux, and the guys wore cream suits with navy blue and gold vests and ties. Savannah's dad married us, and I met Atlas' aunt and uncle, aka mom and dad. The wedding was quick and painless, and we are sitting at the reception having a great time with our friends and family. Peter gave us one of his suites in his hotel in Santorini, Greece, for two weeks. I look over at my husband and reminisce on how so much has changed in this past year or so. I almost died only to be brought back to life by someone who needed to be brought back to life himself. He is my other half, the absolute love of my life.

Everyone clears out, and it's just me and Atlas left in the reception area, and he plays Jess Glynne's I'll Be There, and we have our final dance together alone, to the words of the song that speak of our love for each other. "Come on, baby, the jet is waiting," Atlas says as he sweeps me in his arms and walks us out.

ATLAS'S PLAYLIST

- Next to Me

Imagine Dragons

- Don't Give Up On Me

Andy Grammar

- I Lived

OneRepublic

- Summer Rain

Carl Thomas

- I'll Be There

Jess Glynne

ABOUT THE AUTHOR

J. Nell was born and raised in the city of Rochester, in the fast-paced state of New York. She considers her faith and family to be most important to her. If she isn't spending time with her friends and family you can almost always find her working her full-time job or writing.

She is a self-proclaimed accidental author renowned for her captivating tales of empowered boss black women and the irresistible alphas who fall for them, Author J. Nell weaves stories that transcend boundaries and celebrate love's diverse journey. With a keen eye for exploring both the complexities of modern relationships and the dynamics of cultural diversity.

Author J. Nell creates narratives that resonate deeply with readers, leaving them eagerly turning pages to uncover the enthralling blend of passion, emotion, and personal growth. Her compelling narratives not only entertain but also inspire conversations about love, identity, and the power of breaking societal norms.

Make sure to sign up for J. Nell's Newsletter to find out all the news and exclusives. Salteworkswrites.square.site

twitter.com/author_nell

instagram.com/authorj.nell

amazon.com/author/j.nell

ALSO BY J. NELL

Jag The Gideon Brothers Book 1

Peter The Gideon Brothers and Friends Book 3

Joseph The Gideon Brothers Book 4

The General The Gideon Brothers and Friends Book 6

Anson The Gideon Brothers Book 7

Jaasiel The Gideon Brothers Book 8

JAASIEL
THE GIDEON BROTHERS
J. NELL

Naughty or Nice The Holiday Bad Boys Book 1

Bows & Arrows The Holiday Bad Boys Book 2

Get Lucked The Holiday Bad Boys Book 3

Star Spangled Bondage The Holiday Bad Boys Book 4

Xanthe The Obsidian Brotherhood Book 1

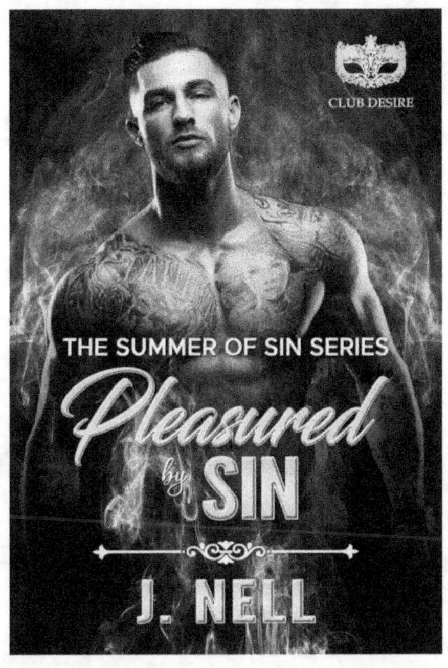

THE SUMMER OF SIN SERIES
Pleasured
by SIN
J. NELL
CLUB DESIRE

9 798988 740087